ENDANGERED
IN THE
OZARKS

Inspired by Actual Events

Sheila Webb Pierson

Dedicated to
those who made me stronger.

Table of Contents

A Note from the Author:

Although this story was inspired by actual events, please keep in mind it is a book of fiction, a product of the author's imagination, and has no historical value whatsoever.

Chapter 1

October 2010

The crisp, October morning air felt exhilarating on his face as he walked up the all-so-familiar trail. He had climbed this trail many times in the past year and a half. The trail always led to two beguiling things, the first being the most breathtaking views he had ever seen.

He recalled standing on the bluff and looking for miles. He could see several slow-flowing streams. After all, he knew there were close to 88,000 miles of streams in Arkansas and over 2,300 named lakes. They were the very heart and soul of the area.

The trees he could see from the bluff provided an ever-changing canvas. Evergreens, such as cedars and elms, populated the rocky terrain, providing a somewhat romantic escape from reality. Cedar trees that couldn't help but spark Christmas memories and inspire holiday aspirations were abundant. The pines grew tall and lean. It seemed they spawned in areas no other tree dared. Pine thickets created groves of land covered with pine needles and, thus, limited underbrush, making it perfect for hiking and camping.

He could also see dozens of fields of a myriad of colors and colorful birds of every kind, including the majestic bald eagle.

Then there was the most beautiful sight he had ever seen, which led to the second beguiling thing: the love of his life.

The solitude of the bluff proved a great escape from the reckless, callous society in which he and she existed. This escape became his favorite sensation to which he looked forward; because during those all-too-brief moments, he was alone with the girl that made him laugh, made him ponder greater things than himself, and made him evaluate good versus evil . . . all in all, she made him a better man. There was no place on Earth where he was ever happier than being in this place with this girl.

On this morning, he watched his steps as he carefully picked his way over the limestone rocks that littered his path. On occasion he would push a low-hanging branch to one side, only to be slapped by another. The cedar trees provided the fresh fragrance that surfaced during his journey. He stopped many times to admire the vivid colors of the leaves clinging to the mighty oak and elm trees for the last few days as the slow march to winter had begun. The red leaves were especially brilliant this year, certainly because of the recent rains. The yellows almost seemed to pay tribute to the commanding reds and, thus, balance the forest.

His pace increased. He couldn't wait to reach the bluff today. He patted his pants pocket to verify his treasure had made the journey up the trail with him, as well. It was so comfortable to wear casual pants and a simple, flannel shirt. He pondered to himself that he needed a job where that attire was common. The typical suits he wore everyday were starting to smother him.

Today would be memorable. He leaned around a strange elm tree shaped like a "Y." They both loved that tree as it was quirky and strong—a bit of symbolism for both of them.

As he reached the top, he gazed at the sheer brilliance of the view. The view was even more striking this morning than he expected. The sun was glowing behind the clouds, leaving an almost cotton-candy effect. He could not have picked a nicer day, and he was filled with excitement.

From the corner of his eye, he saw someone coming. His excitement heightened. He had looked forward to today for months. He had been preparing for the perfect day, the perfect place, the perfect girl, and the perfect question. After months of stress from his work and the true wickedness of the world, today was going to be a respite and reset to what a wonderful life could be. Momentarily, she would be standing next to him.

His anticipation increased until he noticed an unfamiliar form enter through the brushy grove where the trail meandered up the mountain. He stood bewildered, gazing on the form as it slowly materialized in front of him. This was clearly not whom he was expecting. Another form started to materialize behind the first. The first was a larger man with a scowl on his face. The second was a smaller man but menacing, nonetheless. They both moved intentionally toward him.

He started to call out to them, but then a flush of realization came over him. He had an eerie feeling such as he had never felt before. The hairs on his neck stiffened. He recognized them from some of his research, and they were not here to talk. The wickedness had found him.

"Oh, hell," he muttered as he turned and ran from his perch on the bluff.

He heard the steps of the men close in behind him. One grabbed his shirt and pulled him to the ground. He pulled away and sprang up to run again. He ran without direction and soon found himself faced with no escape except upward. He grabbed frantically at the rough rocks to pull himself up; however, the rocks were slick from the morning dew. He was unable to maintain a grip on what seemed to be his only means of escape.

One of the men grabbed him from behind; and this time he threw him to the ground with such a force, the air left his lungs. He lay there defenseless. The man yelled something at him, but it refused to penetrate the fog in his brain. The man thrust a fist into his already breathless chest. He lay there, gasping for breath, for what seemed an eternity. Slowly, his chest began to fill with air again.

Within a few seconds, he found the courage and energy to crawl; however, as he got up on all fours, something hit the side of his head. His ears started ringing. His vision blurred. Falling back to the ground, he cringed in pain. Stretching his arm upward to protect his head from another blow, he felt moisture drenching the side of his face. Pulling his hand down close to his blurry eyes, he saw blood.

He decided he was going to die here. He had to do something or that man was surely going to beat him to death.

He saw one man talking to the other. He could not understand what they were saying. His eyesight all but gone, his head covered in blood, and his lungs still feeling the lack of oxygen, he pulled together his last bit of energy and bolted for the forest. He felt something grab his foot. He was falling. He was reaching for anything that could stop the fall . . . but there was nothing.

Chapter 2

October 2018

"Where are my keys?" Jim stammered.

Digging through the toolbox nestled in the bed of the Arkansas state-issued Ford F150, he stammered again, "Where are those freaking keys? I know I put them here so I wouldn't lose them . . . or did I put them in the house? Wait . . . maybe they are in my pants from yesterday," Jim muttered under his breath when the only living being who could hear him was Jax.

As a 52-year-old biologist, he had worked for over 30 years for the Arkansas Fish and Wildlife Services. While still in his early 20s, Jim found a particular affinity with their mission statement of "conserve, protect, and enhance fish and wildlife habitat to benefit Arkansans" and became passionate about his job. In his 30 years as a biologist, he had become the trusted knowledge source for those unique, special finds and situations.

Jim had a clear understanding that the streams in Arkansas were different than those in the western states. He knew that the aquatic life was much more diverse and that more species of fish were found in one Arkansas stream than all of the species combined in western streams. Understanding that the streams and rivers were home to many aquatic organisms that were under-appreciated and under-protected, he started the Arkansas Stream Team. His love for streams, sparked in his youth, made it only fitting that he spend his adult life protecting these vulnerable and endangered species from current threats.

Jim slammed the lid of the toolbox down and heard a rattle. Yep, the keys were on the lid. Jim grabbed the keys, partly out of frustration and partly out of fear that they would get away from him again. Keys were a struggle for him. Somehow, these tiny, metal, critical instruments seemed to elude him at every moment, often giving him a small panic attack from the fear of being stranded.

"Load up, Jax," muttered Jim as he held the door open for his best friend.

Jax, a four-year-old Australian shepherd, and Jim had become best of pals when Jim rescued Jax two years earlier. He was a quiet and overly well-mannered dog that never barked at anyone. However, he certainly had his way of shaming humans with the auspicious Aussie stare and head tilt. Some thought it cute, but Jim knew that Jax was usually thinking something more like, "Can you please get yourself together? You are embarrassing me."

Fortunately for Jim, Jax was quick to forgive. Jax, loving to ride, quickly gave up his judging look and happily bounded into the passenger seat. Jim started the truck.

"Ok, Jax, let's go caving today."

Jim ruffled the top of Jax's head and reached for his phone for GPS assistance.

"Good grief! Now, where is my phone . . ."

Jax again tilted his head and looked disapprovingly at his master's lack of organization. Jim could feel Jax's disappointment in him and believed he had been a disappointment to Jax for some time. Recently divorced, he had made several decisions to embrace life, rediscovering its many forms . . . some of which would certainly result in disappointing Jax.

His most notable discovery involved his "Gummy Adventure of 2016" while visiting in Colorado, certainly a pivotal moment in Jim's life. Marijuana, still illegal in Arkansas, seemed to be a substance worthy of adventure; but the simple task of finding such a substance at the age of 52 was vexing. Upon deciding he was ready to purchase the next adventure of high, he realized he had no notion of how to track down the proper retail unit. Finally, after moments of thought, he resorted to the best, time-honored method: he asked his waitress at lunch.

"No problem," she replied. "Just go to the corner store, Urban Leaf," she said as she pointed the direction, "and tell the man what type of high you are seeking."

"Type of high?" Jim thought. "Didn't know there were *types* of highs," he jokingly and bewilderingly replied.

The waitress laughed, thinking he was just being silly.

Jim followed the directions from his trusted waitress friend of 45 minutes. Upon entering the store, a gentleman standing behind a glass counter asked, "How can I help you?"

Jim, clearly confused and looking out of place, replied, "I'm not sure."

The store clerk grinned, "From out of state?"

Jim nodded his head and gave an innocent grin, thinking to himself, "Is it that obvious?"

"How do you want to feel?" the store clerk started, then rattled off different options and explained the typical result of each.

Jim thought to himself, "I just want to feel high. How many different high feelings can there be?"

The clerk continued, "There is the low high, and the high, and the I-don't-care high."

Jim, overwhelmed with drug decisions, replied, "Anything but the low high . . . *you* pick."

Jim wondered if it would be a regrettable decision. The store clerk returned with 10 gummies and suggested he start with a kind that promised a bit of a mild, euphoric feeling.

Jim, nervous about his adventure, quickly agreed; paid cash; darted out of the store; and behaving like a criminal, looked both ways before crossing the street to his truck. He recalled how illegal this was back in Arkansas.

Jim returned to the hotel and showered. He planned to attend an afternoon Wildlife Biologists Mixer that was to be held downstairs. After drying off, he glared at the gummies that were in a plastic bag lying on a small table. It seemed they called to him.

Jim sat down on the edge of his bed and read the directions. Remembering the store clerk said these were mild, he decided to eat one. How much trouble could they be in such a tiny dose? Plus, he was not due to be at the mixer for another two hours.

After losing himself into returning emails, Jim suddenly realized it was time to join his colleagues downstairs.

"What a joke these gummies are," Jim thought. "Not one euphoric feeling," he whispered into the mirror while evaluating his five o'clock shadow.

After determining his appearance acceptable, he scurried downstairs to mingle. As Jim arrived at the social event, he took in the view. Around the room stood a variety of people—truly a psychologist's dream. There had to be at least six case studies standing in front of him at any given moment.

To Jim's right stood one of the chiefs. He had over 30 years in at the service, as well. He was pot-bellied, grayed, and loved to tell stories . . . granted every story was about himself; so, his audience was ever-changing. To Jim's left was a younger crowd. These young folks had all graduated within the last three years. They were eagerly sharing some of their findings and aspirations to save the environment.

Jim grabbed a beer from the bar in the corner and joined yet a third set of folks—more seasoned and cynical—whom he had known for years. He listened to the research projects they were leading and how they hoped they would impact the environment in a positive way.

His next memory, however, was that of seeing all his colleagues seated at dinner, looking at him puzzled. He felt as though he was having an out-of-body experience.

His buddy reached over and placed a hand on Jim's shoulder, "Hey . . . are you ok?"

"Of course," Jim replied.

Trying to stifle a giggle, his buddy asked, "By chance, did you partake in some local fun?"

"Why?" Jim asked.

His friend winked and leaned into him to quietly answer, "Because you have asked the same question five times; and each time you ask it, you laugh."

Jim realized he was making the wrong impression among his fellow biologists. However, after a moment of thought, he elected to laugh it up to life lessons learned. He decided to head back to his room . . . now, where was his room key?

Chapter 3

As Jim awoke early one morning a few years later, he was excited about the exploration he had planned for the day. Every day in the wilderness was a joy; that's where Jim found the most peace. Nature was truly a source of solitude for him . . . most days, anyway. Today would be the day to affirm some of his thoughts regarding some very rare and endangered crayfish; however, he did not know if "endangered" would actually be the result of his findings.

Twenty minutes later, he and Jax were on the road headed to the northwest corner of Arkansas to Cherokee City and Spavinaw Creek. The northwest corner of Arkansas borders Missouri and Oklahoma. Missouri, known for its caves and limestone, certainly made for prime conditions to find the caves that housed the elusive, endangered crayfish species.

Unfortunately for Jim, the past had been unkind to him due to his adventurous nature. He respected snakes, especially those found around the water's edge, including the cottonmouth. He also was always on the lookout for the dreaded copperhead. With that being said, his lack of focus often betrayed him.

In July 2007, after taking a quick swim to cool down during a rather long hike, Jim became distracted by a view of an interesting rock formation. Climbing out of the water, he stepped over a small stump to get a better view. While admiring the rocks, he felt what he thought was a branch hit his bare foot. Glancing down before moving, he realized he had, in fact, invaded a copperhead's home. And yes, the copperhead was unhappy with Jim's presence and sent him a message by biting his foot.

Knowing he had no time to waste, Jim abandoned his clothes and jumped in his truck to drive quickly to the hospital. He arrived in pain with a swollen foot and reddish-purple streaks starting up his calf muscle.

The nurse asked if he brought the snake with him. Grimacing in pain he replied, "No, I left him at his house along with my clothes."

The nurse was stressed that, without the snake, she would not be able to identify the proper anti-venom she should use.

Jim responded, "No worries . . . I am a biologist, and I have no doubt that it was a copperhead."

The nurse almost appeared disappointed or unconvinced, as if a half-naked man who claimed to be a biologist would have stepped into a copperhead haven. Was he truly a biologist or a meth abuser who didn't know where he was or that he had made a bad step? Regardless, Jim was treated and remained in ICU for three days.

In July 2011, Jim had returned from work one late afternoon. He had felt badly all day. He was unnaturally tired; he had a throbbing headache; and his muscles ached like he had the flu. When he stepped out of his truck, he fell flat on the gravel driveway. He woke up 24 hours later in ICU where he spent the rest of the week.

"Rocky Mountain Spotted Tick Fever," the semi-annoyed nurse recited as to why he was in the hospital. Jim was in and out of consciousness for several days. By the time he was released, he had lost muscle tone along with 12 pounds, as well as his respect for the nursing profession.

Then there was July 2014. Jim decided to attend a free, local concert for which a little group from Louisiana would be headlining. He set up his favorite camp chair that had been stored in his garage for the past four months. This was his "going-to-town" chair as it was less ratted and more suitable for the public to see and prevent his being accused of living in depravity.

The music was disappointing . . . so much so, he slumped in his chair and reached for his drink. Quickly the slump turned into a sharp pain on his exposed arm. He shook it violently and realized he had laid his arm on a brown recluse, and it was expressing its dissatisfaction for being carted to a subpar folk music concert. That little acquaintance with the spider resulted in yet another trip to the hospital and a long recovery from rotting skin over the summer. He felt certain people thought he had leprosy as the bite healed.

There was more: July 2015 found him viewing himself as already a blood brother to snakes, ticks, and spiders. However, he was proven wrong yet again, succumbing to another "microscopic militia." He was diagnosed with Lyme disease.

"Good grief," Jim thought. "July sucks. It would be better to just skip that month every year."

Jim began to think he might be wise to save vacation time and take a full month off in a condo in New England. It seemed the safest option. However, he was not sure he could be away from the beauty of the Ozarks that long.

At some point, a person had to wonder if Jim's blood, being so tainted by all the infections that nature had bestowed on him, would actually kill a tick if it bit him.

Then the adventures of 2018 began . . .

*****

Jim and Jax bounced along a stretch of dirt road, nearing the Oklahoma line. Jim took in all the beautiful landscape. He had waited more than 15 years to explore a special cave located on the property on which he now drove. During that time, Huck Ferguson had owned the property. This cave had the perfect conditions to house the precious, ever-allusive crayfish. Jim had requested permission to explore the cave every year for those 15 years . . . and every year for those 15 years he had been denied by Huck.

Huck Ferguson was a commodity broker in Arkansas specializing in corn, soybeans, and other commodity contracts. He had made a mint as he seemed to have a second sense of how the commodity market would swing. He lived in Little Rock for the most part. At some point, he purchased a parcel of land near Cherokee City as a hunting retreat for himself and his clients. He built a spectacular log cabin, which had been used at times for large parties he was known to host.

This particular section of land was very grassy, edged by a deep, dense forest and, of course, had a stream running through the western threshold. The trees had become a perfect haven for deer and wildlife, which attracted some of Huck's very influential friends. Using this property as a tool, Huck had managed to build rapport with the movers and shakers of Arkansas. He often used the cabin as a way to meet, mingle, and influence the elite and political powers of Arkansas.

Cherokee City was a community with very few residents. However, it lay only ten miles from Siloam Springs, Arkansas, nestled on the Oklahoma-Arkansas border. In the late 1800s it was known as a place to find healing powers from the natural springs.

Huck enjoyed his secluded cabin for years but frequented the town of Siloam Springs, mostly for supplies but also for neighborly socializing from time-to-time.

Suddenly, something changed. Huck seemed to have retreated from the world, and his daughter took charge. It had only been a year ago when she sold the country cabin to Charlie and Rebecca Moore.

The Moores were not originally from Arkansas. In fact, they were from Kansas City, Missouri. As a retired couple, they purchased the estate so they could fulfill a life-long dream of owning a small farm, as well as move closer to their grandchildren who lived in nearby Bentonville.

When Jim requested permission to explore the cave yet one more time . . . only this time from the new owners . . . the Moores blissfully agreed. The Moores gave Jim permission to explore the cave at will. They truly loved their surroundings and were fascinated by the possibility that Jim's team might find an endangered species on their property.

Jim's team was scheduled to meet him at the cave. He had three biologists who worked for him scaling the streams of Arkansas, searching for fish species to record and monitor. They recorded population numbers, general health of the fish, and documented any contaminants that would harm the continued survival of the species.

During their journey as the "Stream Team," they had already discovered an endangered crayfish and identified a native smallmouth bass that was decreasing in population and range rather quickly. Although they always wanted their anglers to appreciate and enjoy their experiences, Jim's Stream Team was very devoted to protecting the fish and their environment.

Jim continued on the dusty, dirt road, hitting every pothole it seemed. Jax enjoyed the air hitting his face as he perched on the armrest of the passenger door and extended his head out the window. The fast-moving air pushed the Aussie's massive mane behind him as he closed his eyes, enjoying the sensation.

The GPS informed Jim he was to turn right in 200 feet. He slowed and started looking for the turn. He noticed a simple, cottage-style house snuggled off the road. The cottage had a wraparound porch, very southern in style. Rocking on the porch in a solid, wooden rocking chair was a middle-aged woman with blonde hair flowing down around her shoulders. She wore a T-shirt and jeans and nothing on her feet. Her light complexion made her stand out. She appeared to be working on a laptop while enjoying the cool, morning air.

Jim caught her catching him looking at her. He smirked out of embarrassment and waved. She promptly lit up a brilliant smile and waved back . . . a smile that seemed contagious to Jim as he couldn't help but smile back. Then she lowered her gaze back to the screen she had been viewing. Jim was almost sad the smile ended and very nearly missed his turn.

Chapter 4

Jim arrived at the Moore home. He stepped out of his truck and was quickly greeted by Charlie and Rebecca. The other biologists on his team had already arrived and were standing around talking, each with some kind of pastry in their hand. The Moores, as well as the biologists, were full of excitement that Jim's Stream Team might very well uncover a hidden treasure right on their property.

Rebecca was a sweet woman. She was small in stature but possessed a booming laugh. She ushered Jim to the side of the house where she had set up homemade snacks and water for his team.

"Oh, Mrs. Moore, you have done way too much for us," Jim acknowledged with the most appreciation.

"Nonsense," Rebecca replied. "You boys will need a boost to do all that work today. It's truly a pleasure for me."

Jim smiled at her as he had never been received by property owners with so much enthusiasm.

Seeing Mr. Moore approach from around the house, Jim took the opportunity to extend his thanks to him, as well. "Mr. Moore, again, I want to thank you and your wife for allowing us on your property for some exploration."

"Not a problem. It will be quite a story for us to tell our grandkids, who are coming over later today, I dare say," Charlie replied in a jovial and eager manner.

"Come on, Jax," Jim hollered, giving Jax the command for which he had been waiting.

Jax leaped out of the truck and raced to Jim. Along the way, he subsequently sniffed Charlie and Rebecca before lowering his guard as the fiercest dog known to man. Charlie sneaked Jax a little bite of a blueberry muffin and patted his back roughly. That was all it took for Jax to decide Charlie was now his new best friend.

Jim's team started unloading their equipment from their truck, which consisted of seining nets, snorkel equipment, thermometers, water test kits, headlamps, and flashlights. It promised to be a primitive operation at best but perfect for an ancient cave.

In single file, the biologists climbed down to the stream, which was only about 200 yards from the cabin. Charlie and Rebecca stayed perched at the edge of the yard, watching the team descend. It was a rough descent as the hills had become overgrown in briars; poison ivy; tall, Johnson grass; and thistles. However, this was certainly not uncommon for the team, and they were prepared.

They waded into the stream and started expanding out their nets and equipment. They carefully waded toward the cave for which they all had eagerly awaited exploring. The experience of the team taught them to be sure-footed and careful as to what habitat they disrupted on their journey, even before their feet actually hit the water.

The Stream Team turned a bend in the stream and discovered the small cave a short distance away. They continued to slowly creep closer and closer, observing the natural setting and stopping from time to time to make notes of interesting findings which might lead them to that coveted, rare discovery.

The cave was at the base of a large, steep, layered bluff, likely 40-50 feet high. The majestic rocks had been eaten by water thousands of years ago to leave only a maze of crevices. The mossy layers stood as a slight fortress against the elements. The moss was as vibrant green as the greens only found on the eighteenth hole at Augusta.

Jim arrived at the mouth of the cave first. Having had experience with snakes, he took the precautions of surveying the area closely for them since they were known to frequent cave openings. Passing inspection, Jim continued his creep. Turning on his headlamp, he carefully slid into the mouth of the cave on his knees and made more passes of light with a flashlight to verify safe entrance. Again, inspection proved acceptable.

Jim slid completely into the cave, although unable to stand erect because of the low ceiling. He made more quick passes of light. Noticing the area seemed free from danger, he gave the okay for the Stream Team to follow. While waiting for Jim's okay, the Stream Team had slipped on hard hats, knee pads, and headlamps so as to speed up the entry and research.

The cave was wet and cold . . . a great reprieve from the humid and hot weather of recent days. The walls were slimy, documenting where high water had settled during the spring months. The cave had no inlet of light. It was dark and ominous. It was perfect!

At the far end of the tiny cave, Jim noticed another opening. He was excited to explore it; but that needed to wait as a seemingly insignificant pool of water, certain to house an endangered species, was within reach. He instructed his Stream Team to start moving slowly through the small pool of water. Following their boss's lead, they spread out and moved very deliberately, trying not to disturb the fine sediment distributed across the bottom of the pool.

Curiosity getting the better of him, Jim eventually crawled up the rocks to the second cave opening he had discovered earlier. Throwing light into the dark fortress, he noticed what first appeared to be nothing more than a layer of rocks that water seldom, if ever, reached. He started to turn his attention back to his team of young biologists when his light lit on a formation that both excited him and scared him all at the same time. Catching his breath, Jim lowered the light and took yet another look. Was he just seeing things?

"For the love of God, what is this?" Jim's voice echoed through the cave.

Realizing that there was a different tone to their superior's voice, the more senior biologist jumped to Jim's side, expecting to see a miracle of nature. However, both breathlessly dropped to a sitting position and simply stared: they were looking at a skeleton . . . an adult human skeleton.

The human bones seemed to have remained untouched by human or animal for some time. Nonetheless, the bones were not smooth to the touch, indicating the skeleton had been exposed to erosion. Jim instructed the Stream Team to continue their work in the lower level of the cave and not to reenter the tomb of the unknown human.

Jim carefully slid back out of the cave and into the stream. He waded back through the flowing water to the bank which led to his truck. Jax was waiting patiently at the stream's edge, but seemed hesitant to climb back into the truck as if to say to Jim, "You have not been gone long enough for my nap."

Jim could see Charlie and Rebecca in the distance and gave them a quick wave. In his head he began to formulate what he would tell them. They were already in a heightened mode, and this was not going to help calm them in the least.

Jim went directly to his truck and picked up his cell phone, ready to call the police and report . . . what? As Jim rehearsed a possible speech in his head, he dialed 9-1-1. When the call would not go through, he stared at the phone's screen: there was not enough cell coverage to make a call.

Eagerly pacing the yard of the cabin, the Moores wondered if Jim had found the species, yet. As soon as Jim turned from his truck and returned to the cabin, they crowded around him.

"Did you find anything exciting in the cave?" Charlie eagerly quizzed Jim, his eyebrows raised in a questioning expression.

"Nope, not yet," Jim answered calmly, wondering if a human skeleton would fall under "anything exciting." "Just gotta make a quick call right now," he added, holding up his phone as an indication. "I wanted to let you know I gotta go find a signal, but I'll be back shortly."

He and Jax jumped in his truck, cell phone in hand, and headed back down the same dirt road until a signal could be found. Luckily for him, he found a good signal just outside the little cottage that had housed the pretty lady on the porch earlier.

He placed his call to the police and explained to them his "find" in the cave. After a short conversation with the deputy sheriff of Benton County, Jim turned his truck around and started his journey back to the Moores' cabin. As he passed the cottage with the wraparound porch, he glanced over to it again, somewhat hoping to see the pretty lady; but this time he was out of luck.

"What a day this has been," Jim muttered to Jax, "and it's only 10 a.m."

Jax was too busy scratching burrs to notice Jim's discontent.

Chapter 5

Deputy Sheriff Homer Biggs arrived at the Moores' cabin about 20 minutes later. Jim motioned for Charlie and Rebecca to join him and the deputy and explained to all three of them at the same time what he had found. The three men set out to climb down toward the stream for a better look. Homer was convinced Jim was simply the victim of a prank.

Homer had grown up in Decatur, Arkansas. A young man of only 28 years, Homer was blessed, in a certain sense, that he lived in a relatively crime-free area. His biggest case to date was uncovering a small meth lab in an abandoned mobile home. Unfortunately, Homer had been unable to identify the owners.

Although young and somewhat inexperienced, Homer had the confidence of a 40-year-old veteran. He repeatedly told Jim he should not be worried about being embarrassed by a prank, that these things happened all the time.

Jim carefully guided Homer and Charlie down the stream and into the cave while Rebecca waited on the bank. As they passed the busy biologists, Homer prudently noted the careful work in which the Stream Team was engaged. Out of his element in the cave, he slipped and slid and quickly became slightly claustrophobic.

Upon reaching their destination, Jim pointed out the skeleton. Homer quickly started reciting the many ways to determine whether a skeleton was real or fake. Upon implementing each factual statement, Homer began to sense that the skeleton was, in fact, real. The sudden realization that he was actually looking at and touching a bonafide skeleton sent a nauseous stir through Homer's body. Jim quickly realized Homer's dilemma and swiftly ushered him out into the fresh air.

Homer regained his faculties after splashing a little cold stream water on his face. He gave Jim a lost look. Sensing that Homer was in over his head and not wanting to embarrass him, Jim suggested to him that they retreat back to the cabin and make a few phone calls for assistance. Homer eagerly accepted the suggestion and followed Jim to the patrol car.

By the time Homer, Jim, and Charlie made it back to the patrol car, Homer had regained his sense of responsibility. Homer prudently radioed in a call to the sheriff, Zeke Drennan.

"Sheriff, we have a dead body. It is in a cave on Charlie and Rebecca Moore's property," he said, putting his recently lost confidence back into his voice. "Arkansas Fish and Wildlife is up here doing some work in the cave and discovered the body."

Almost as though the discovery of the skeleton was an inconvenience, Sheriff Drennan hesitantly answered Homer, "A dead body on the Moore property? I'll be there in about 20." As an afterthought, he instinctively instructed Homer, "I need you to immediately seal off that cave and keep everyone, including Fish and Wildlife, out of there until further notice."

Jim cringed at the words . . . words that brought disappointment to Jim's ears. Jim knew that the discovery of the skeleton would likely be the only discovery for that day.

Sheriff Drennan arrived on the scene in true southern-sheriff fashion. After stepping out of his immaculate truck—rather than a patrol car—he pulled his cowboy hat over his crew-cut head. Bearded, over six feet tall, fit, grimacing, gun on his side, sunglasses . . . he was a very intimidating-looking man. He approached Homer.

"Deputy Biggs, take me to your scene," he commanded in a straight-forward demeanor.

Homer anxiously glanced at Jim, his eyes pleading for his help.

Jim quickly picked up on his signal and graciously proposed, "I can show you to the cave."

"Sure, as soon as you tell me who you are," replied Sheriff Drennan.

Homer quickly spoke up, "Sheriff Drennan, this is Jim Cunningham with Arkansas Fish and Wildlife. He is the one who found the skeleton."

The sheriff shook Jim's hand and succinctly said, "Proceed."

Upon their arrival at the cave entrance, Sheriff Drennan gave a large sigh as his fears were confirmed: he was going to have to crawl through the space. The three entered the cave as Jim assisted them with guidance and light.

Sheriff Drennan sat on the cave floor for a moment getting used to the lack of light. Then he agreeably followed Jim to the upper level of the cave and did, in fact, verify what Jim and Homer had already known: there was a human skeleton. Sheriff Drennan motioned for the three of them to exit.

After wading back through the creek and stepping onto the dry bank, Sheriff Drennan informed his deputy, "Homer, I've already called the Arkansas State Police, and their crime lab team is enroute."

It was clear to see that Homer was considerably jumpier in the presence of his boss.

"Yes, Sir . . . good thinking," Homer replied.

Sheriff Drennan smirked toward Homer and quipped, "I thought so." Sheriff Drennan then turned his attention to Jim and inquired, "So why are you here, again?"

Jim chuckled a little and then retold the story of exploring for endangered crayfish. The answer did not seem to impress the embodiment of the law walking in the lead back to the truck.

Upon reaching the truck, Sheriff Drennan updated the Moores, "We have State Police on their way. There is, in fact, a human skeleton in the cave down there. I ask for your patience as the crime lab team arrives soon to tag and bag the scene."

They nodded their heads in agreement, their eyes wide with surprise.

"Of course," Rebecca said as she finally found her voice. "We understand." She thrust out her arm toward the table of snacks and water she had set up for the biologists as she offered, "Please help yourself to some snacks and water. We have plenty more inside. We don't want any of you to become dehydrated."

The sheriff nodded his head in appreciation.

Jim returned to his truck to check on Jax whom he found to be napping in the shade nearby. The excitement didn't seem to disturb him much.

Moments later, a van pulled in, and three people stepped out. A striking, Native American woman approached Sheriff Drennan. She stood as tall as he did and displayed a very serious look on her face. A badge hung around her neck; her dark hair was pulled back tightly into a neat bun. She was fit, slender, and had piercing, dark eyes.

Jim thought to himself, "Tall people seem to promote well in the Arkansas State Police system."

Sheriff Drennan suddenly motioned for Jim to rejoin them.

"Detective Lori Garringer, this is Mr. Cunningham. He found the remains this morning. Mr. Cunningham, this is Detective Garringer. She has some questions for you."

Detective Garringer proceeded to ask Jim the same questions that Homer and Sheriff Drennan had already asked. At this point, there was no emotion left in Jim's answers other than frustration by the fact that they couldn't seem to write down his answers.

Detective Garringer and her crime scene team followed Jim as he, once again, waded through the stream to the cave. The Stream Team assisted with the massive amount of equipment that needed to be transported to the cave for the crime scene team. Soon, the crime scene team began the detailed process of measuring, sampling, and bagging evidence.

After the crime scene team started their work, Jim pulled his team aside, "Folks, I apologize, but this is the only discovery for today. Take our gear and head back to town. I'll see if we can get clearance to try again at a later date."

Jim stuck around and chatted with the Moores and Sheriff Drennan while the crime scene team worked. Sheriff Drennan seemed to loosen up after getting to know the spectators better. He even smiled at least twice . . . almost a record for him.

Detective Garringer returned from the cave several hours later, unannounced and almost unnoticed during a jovial conversation about the Razorback football team.

"Sheriff Drennan, we have completed our process," Detective Garringer inserted. "I will send you the information upon review from the Medical Examiner at the State Crime Lab."

"Thank you, Detective Garringer. I look forward to the report."

Sheriff Drennan then shook the detective's hand as she turned to leave. With all the excitement seeming to end with that simple gesture, Jim excused himself, along with Sheriff Drennan. He climbed in his truck as the sheriff climbed into his and, with Jax riding shotgun, he followed the sheriff's truck down the lane.

Chapter 6

Moments later, Sheriff Drennan parked in front of his office, which was situated next to the jail in Bentonville. He stepped out of his truck and started to walk toward the sliding doors into the brick and glass building. Suddenly, he heard quick steps racing up from behind him.

Just as the sheriff turned toward the sound of the footsteps, Homer stopped next to him and fired off, "So, who do you think it was? Do you think the news station will go out there for a story? Do you think they will want to interview me . . . er, I mean *you?*"

Sheriff Drennan, in completely irritated fashion, responded, "No!"

Homer gave a confused look but made the wise decision to leave the sheriff alone. He stopped and allowed the sheriff to continue on into the building.

As Drennan walked into his office, he nodded to his office manager, Opal, who was seated at her desk, working through a stack of reports, checking for any errors. Opal, a woman in her 60s, was a very capable woman who ran the sheriff's office like a well-oiled machine. She was nearly as sarcastic as Sheriff Drennan with her scowling look that intimidated nearly everyone she met.

"How'd it go?" Opal asked, barely looking up at the sheriff.

Sheriff Drennan responded, "It's a skeleton. Someone had a bad day . . . just don't know who yet."

Homer came up behind Sheriff Drennan and piped up, "Ms. Opal, it beat all you ever saw . . . a full human skeleton . . . like it had never been touched—like a man sleeping!"

Opal looked up over her stack of cumbersome papers and said, "Anyone you know?"

Caught off guard, Homer answered, "I don't know yet. The crime lab came in and bagged and tagged."

Opal's gaze returned to her work just as Sheriff Drennan shut his office door. Homer decided he needed to get to his reports while the details were still fresh in his mind and casually stepped toward the bull pen where the deputies worked.

Sheriff Drennan tossed his hat on a filing cabinet and took a seat in his frayed, rocking desk chair and stared out the window. The view from his window was terrible. The parking lot was full of worn-out department cars. The parking lot itself was recently resurfaced but already showing decay and cracks. The Arkansas summers were so brutally hot that the structures in this area were quick to show reactive distress.

Sheriff Drennan's office was one of clutter. He had a nice, built-in bookshelf that housed years of interesting books. Surprisingly, Drennan loved to read. He didn't care for criminal fiction but, instead, liked history. His favorite books included *Truman, Reclaiming History (JFK Assassination),* and *Ghost Wars.* Although he had read them many times, they took front and center in his massive collection.

Behind his desk was situated a credenza loaded with binders and bundles of paper . . . reports that had recently been filed or were needing to be filed. Drennan, although very tech savvy, often preferred the feel of paper while reading his reports for details.

Drennan sat, staring into the glare of the sun that bounced off the asphalt.

"I guess this will be another investigation to add to this pile of bureaucracy," he thought to himself.

He decided to grab some water and face this investigation head-on. He headed out of the office to the break room for some fresh, cold water. Apparently, Homer had a similar idea as Sheriff Drennan found him standing at the refrigerator seizing a bottle of water.

"Care for a water?" Homer asked as he offered the sheriff a bottle.

"Sure," Sheriff Drennan replied.

"Sheriff," Homer timidly began, "you know those caves are haunted, right?"

Sheriff Drennan finished his first gulp of cold water and looked at Homer with a frown. Homer, although young, had an amazing work ethic and truly was quite clever with forensics. However, he also could be rather gullible and even naïve, indicative of his age and inexperience.

"Haunted?" Sheriff Drennan repeated sarcastically.

"Yeah," Homer began. "My mom told me for years to never go to the caves along Spavinaw Creek. She said there is so much history surrounding outlaws using those caves for cover or as a place to leave their loot for friends or for themselves when they would return later."

Sheriff Drennan threw Homer a questioning glance.

"No kidding! Jesse James, Belle Star, and Pretty Boy Floyd were all said to have hidden in those caves!" Homer added breathlessly.

Sheriff Drennan continued to stare at Homer with no emotion.

Homer continued, "In fact, there used to be treasure hunters exploring the caves while I was in high school."

"Where did you go to high school?" Sheriff Drennan asked, hoping to deflect the subject.

"Oh, sure . . . uh, Decatur . . . only 20 minutes from here," Homer replied. "I forget you haven't been here but a few years."

Sheriff Drennan smirked as he took another big gulp from his water.

"So, why do you think the caves are haunted, Homer?"

The sheriff's voice sounded almost taunting, but Homer did not catch the barb in Sheriff Drennan's question and became excited again. He started fidgeting with the cups of utensils on the counter.

"Because there are sounds in the caves . . . and lights!"

"Sounds? Lights?" Drennan repeated as he nodded towards Homer.

If a nod could be sarcastic, Sheriff Drennan had mastered the skill.

"Yes, like laughter but then like moans," Homer continued. "A . . . an . . . and the lights are more like a small glow!" Homer stammered as he dropped a cup full of plastic forks to the floor.

"And how . . . pray tell . . . would you know these insightful things?" Sheriff Drennan pitched back to Homer while rubbing his brow from watching the disastrous fumbling of the forks.

The thought raced through Sheriff Drennan's head, "This man, who cannot handle a cup of plastic forks, is armed."

Without voicing the thought, the sheriff shook his head.

"Well, I didn't want to say anything," Homer started, "but when I was in high school, my buddy, Chad, and I sneaked out there one night after a football game."

"How was it?" Sheriff Drennan asked.

"Oh, we won that night. We won big in overtime," Homer responded pragmatically.

Sheriff Drennan stood there staring at Homer, not believing what he was hearing.

Homer, catching the astonished glare from Sheriff Drennan, quickly corrected himself, "I mean, after the game we decided to see what all the fuss was about in the caves. Chad and I were extra stealthy and hiked up to the cave near the Anderson farm."

"And . . ." Sheriff Drennan prodded slightly, flaying his arms.

"Oh . . . well . . . once we were there, we heard some sounds in the caves and could see a glow. Chad got a little scared, so we left. I didn't want my momma finding out I was up there. I was more afraid of her than whatever was in that cave," Homer summed.

"Ever return?" Sheriff Drennan asked.

"Nope . . . not a chance!" Homer replied.

"Anderson's farm, you say?" Sheriff Drennan asked.

Homer nodded.

"Maybe I should follow up on any recent activity," Sheriff Drennan said as he walked out of the break room.

He looked back to see Homer still fidgeting with the forks.

"Maybe you should get back to work, as well, Homer," Sheriff Drennan strongly suggested.

At that statement, Homer dropped the forks a second time. Sheriff Drennan took a deep breath, shook his head, and returned to his office.

Back in his comfy desk chair, Sheriff Drennan found himself deep in thought.

"Haunted caves . . ." he mumbled. "What would someone mistake for being haunted?" Sheriff Drennan thought as he rocked his chair. "Anderson . . ." Sheriff Drennan spoke softly as he continued his thought.

"Well, if there were any suspicious activities or trespassing on Anderson's farm, then we should have a record," Sheriff Drennan said as he aggressively moved toward his keyboard and logged in to the department dispatch program.

He searched for trespassing cases. After reviewing a long list of complaints, he excluded all but a dozen or so claims in the last four years. These cases needed a little more digging, but none referenced caves of any kind.

Then Sheriff Drennan searched for suspicious person complaints. Just as he had suspected, there were only ten or so in four years. This area seemed to be a very safe place to live, which is why the discovery of the skeleton was such a shock. The most surprising discovery was there was nothing noted near Anderson's farm on Spavinaw.

Sheriff Drennan continued to stare at the screen for a few minutes, rubbing his rather square jaw. Suddenly, he stood; grabbed his hat; and left his office, walking toward Ms. Opal's desk.

"I'll be out for a while, Opal," Sheriff Drennan announced.

Opal didn't even bother looking up from her mountain of responsibility. She instinctively waved her hand, not certain or caring if Sheriff Drennan saw her effort.

Chapter 7

Sheriff Drennan stepped into his truck and drove west out of town and headed to the Anderson farm. As he approached the farm, he paid special attention to any landscapes that seemed suitable for caves. Spavinaw Creek was too far from the road to really see any clues . . . and that was, in itself, a huge, red flag for Sheriff Drennan.

He drove up the dirt driveway toward the Anderson house. The road was full of puddles of water from a recent rain. Typically, Sheriff Drennan was one to care about the appearance of his patrol truck but not today. He hit the puddles with attitude and splashed fresh mud onto the doors and sides of his truck.

The sheriff parked and exited his truck as he noticed Bill Anderson stepping out of his barn. The barn was a lofty, metal building that Sheriff Drennan was certain was used as a shop for his tractors, which explained the tall, garage doors.

"Bill," Sheriff Drennan started, "how are things going?"

Sheriff Drennan stuck his hand out for a greeting and was met with Bill Anderson's firm handshake. Sheriff Drennan noticed the strength and noted that farmers typically had a solid handshake after dealing with equipment all day.

"Fine. Wasn't expecting to see you out here. Any problems, Sheriff?" Bill questioned.

"Not really. I'm just following up on some trespassing issues," Sheriff Drennan answered. "By chance, have you had any trouble over the last . . . say . . . four years regarding trespassing?"

"Yeah, as a matter of fact, I've had loads of trouble. About time somebody elevated my complaints," he stated and stepped back, crossing his arms.

Sheriff Drennan noticed the sudden change in Bill's demeanor.

"Have you made complaints, Bill?" Sheriff Drennan inquired with an astonished look.

"Yes, I've made numerous complaints—for years!" Bill continued, working himself into an annoyed state. "As a matter of fact, I have kept record of the complaints."

"You've kept a record?" Sheriff Drennan repeated and inquired at the same time.

"Yes. I decided you guys were never going to respond, so I thought I would start plotting the times I had trespassers and see if I could find a pattern . . . you know, who was coming through town during those days, if it was payday, or even if it was associated with high school games." Anderson talked while he walked, then motioned for Sheriff Drennan to follow him into the barn. "However, I never could piece together anything of substance."

Bill continued to talk as the two walked through his barn littered with tractor parts. Sheriff Drennan, being used to that scene, never lost step behind Anderson. Anderson reached the wall where he clearly kept a series of power tool charging stations, tools, a few tractor manuals covered in oil, and a notebook. He picked up the notebook, turned several pages back, and handed it to Sheriff Drennan.

"This is my record of trespassers," Bill stated as he watched Sheriff Drennan for a reaction.

Sheriff Drennan reviewed the pages in a bit of astonishment.

"Bill, why didn't you call any of these in?"

"Why didn't I call them in?" Bill repeated, clearly irritated. "I called every one of those in," he firmly stated as he jabbed his index finger in the direction of the notebook.

Sheriff Drennan peered up over the notebook to meet Anderson's eyes. They were determined and narrowed. A large vein blossomed over his brow. Sheriff Drennan knew he was serious. He then decided to take pictures of all of Anderson's notes with his phone.

"When you called these in, who answered?" Sheriff Drennan inquired.

"Mostly Kyle Foster, but there were others. In fact, Kyle was always the one who came out to investigate. He seemed pretty diligent about it. He would stop in and let me know he was checking into any issues. Then about an hour later, he would let me know he found some kids around or maybe there was nobody around. I appreciated his effort but couldn't understand how he couldn't arrest the culprits. I just assumed he was a tad incompetent . . . I mean at his age and all."

Sheriff Drennan leaned against the somewhat-gutted tractor while he listened to Bill. After Bill had completed his recollection, Sheriff Drennan thanked him for his time and assured him he would personally check into his records and would have a talk with Kyle.

As Sheriff Drennan reentered his truck, failing to avoid the mud, his mind raced. "Trespassers in the caves, complaints filed but neither recorded into the dispatch system nor followed up, and only Kyle investigated," he thought to himself.

Sheriff Drennan did not like where his mind was going. On the way back to town, he made a quick call to Opal. "Opal, off the record," Sheriff Drennan initiated as a code.

"Off the record," she repeated.

"Do you know of any issues with Kyle lately?"

"Not really . . . only that he seems to miss a lot of work," Opal responded matter-of-factly.

"Really? I was unaware. Like, how much work has he missed?"

"Oh, it seems it comes in spurts. Some months he is fine; other months he is off maybe a day every week," Opal responded.

"Could you print out a report of Kyle's time-off requests and put it on my desk? Oh, and I'm going home," Sheriff Drennan remarked as he hung up.

Chapter 8

Sheriff Drennan backed his patrol truck into his carport and stepped out, again not avoiding the mud and gunk on his truck door. Before shutting the door, he stretched his back as tension had started settling in his joints.

He stepped through his back door into his kitchen. He could smell something baking in the oven, like an herb-and-cheese dish.

"Damn," he said.

His wife, Ashley, tried new recipes regularly . . . and failed regularly. He had learned that a dish smelling good was no indication of its taste. Accepting his fate, he removed his boots onto the tile floor, set his hat on the hook by the door, and walked into the living room. There sat Ashley reading another romance novel. She peered up as he entered the room.

"You are home early."

"Yes, I had some work to do down by Spavinaw; so, I thought I would call it an early day and come home for some lovin'."

As he said that, he glanced over to Ashley who returned the sentiment with a frown and a quick "Ha!"

He took a seat in his recliner and let out a healthy sigh.

"What seems to be bothering you?" Ashley asked as she laid her book down in her lap.

"Oh, nothing . . . just trying to figure out if something is wrong with Kyle. I'm a little concerned he has a health issue."

"Oh, that explains it," Ashley said as she picked up her book to resume her reading.

"Explains what?" Sheriff Drennan asked as if he had been challenged.

"Oh, nothing. I heard about three years or so ago that Kyle was battling a drug addiction. If he were sick, that would make sense," Ashley concluded, never taking her eyes off the page of her book.

Sheriff Drennan sat in his recliner consuming what he had heard. Drug use on his force was a terminable offense.

He got up and walked straight through the kitchen, slipped on his boots, and grabbed his hat. Ashley was saying something about dinner almost being ready, but he had something he needed to deal with. Sheriff Drennan did not bother responding to Ashley but simply walked out the door and started to climb into his muddy truck.

"Where did all this mud come from?" he muttered as he stepped up onto the running board of his truck.

After arriving back at the office, Sheriff Drennan decided to walk in through the back door, which was a rare thing for him to do. He slithered through the office of night deputies, not making eye contact or greeting any of them.

"Good evenin'," Deputy Lane started before he realized Sheriff Drennan was not in a communicative state of mind.

Sheriff Drennan made eye contact with Kyle Foster as he moved through the office area. Kyle started to say something, but years of detective work gave him pause.

Sheriff Drennan stepped into his office. He again tossed his hat on a filing cabinet and plummeted himself into his desk chair. There on his desk was a manila folder from Opal, just as he expected. He quickly opened the folder and scanned the details.

There were dates and dates of Deputy Foster's leave requests. Sheriff Drennan penciled in numbers and days of the week, trying to find a pattern . . . nothing. He then leaned back and rocked slightly in his chair. Staring at the ceiling afforded him the blank space that allowed him to think.

Suddenly, he stopped all motion, jolted to a sitting position, and started digging in his pockets for his phone. He pulled up Bill Anderson's notes. The dates from the complaints filed by Anderson were always one day before Kyle's leave request.

The sudden realization of a pattern hit Sheriff Drennan. He started to suspect Kyle of being involved in something criminal, but he needed confirmation. Sheriff Drennan left his chair in haste and stepped into the hallway. He almost jogged to the deputy bull pen area where the night deputies sat.

"Deputy Lane, would you follow me?" Sheriff Drennan commanded.

Deputy Lane quickly jumped to a standing position and hastily followed Sheriff Drennan back into his office. They both entered the office, and Sheriff Drennan closed the door; but neither took a seat.

"Deputy Lane," Sheriff Drennan started, "I need some straight-up answers."

Deputy Lane nodded in confirmation while shaking just slightly.

"Have you noticed anything unusual about Deputy Kyle Foster?"

Deputy Lane clearly became uncomfortable as he started fidgeting in his stance, slightly rocking back and forth.

"Sheriff, Deputy Foster is my boss. I'm uncomfortable with this discussion," Deputy Lane very diplomatically finally responded.

"And I'm *his* boss. This is not a request for information; this is an *order*," Sheriff Drennan responded while staring down into Deputy Lane's eyes with sheer determination.

Deputy Lane took a minute and carefully responded, "Yes, sir. I have noticed subtle changes in Deputy Foster's behavior. Some nights he would return from a call and seem to be slightly confused and, yet, euphoric. He often had dilated eyes. Sheriff Drennan, if I didn't know better, I would say he was high on something."

Not expecting this answer—especially so easily—Sheriff Drennan was caught off guard. Keeping his eyes on Deputy Lane's eyes, he simply nodded in understanding.

"And you chose not to report this?" he finally quizzed.

"Yes, sir, I can see this was a mistake . . . I truly *did* consider it, but Deputy Foster has always told us that if there were issues, they came to him and him alone."

Sheriff Drennan shook his head, beginning to get a clearer picture of the situation.

"Deputy Lane, you can return to your station; but stay close. And no, there will be no disciplinary action toward you if you are worried."

Deputy Lane took a deep breath, relieved by the sheriff's statement. Then he quickly exited the office faster than he had entered.

"Deputy Foster," Sheriff Drennan bellowed, "join me in my office."

Deputy Foster was in an office no more than 50 feet from Drennan's. He quickly got up, adjusted his uniform, and headed towards the sheriff's office. He glanced toward the bull pen and noted that all the night deputies were looking toward him with the exception of Deputy Lane, who just sat down. Deputy Foster started running different scenarios through his head as he approached Sheriff Drennan's office.

He arrived at the sheriff's office to see Sheriff Drennan sitting behind his desk with his head resting in his right hand.

"Shut the door, and take a seat," the sheriff commanded in a very directive tone.

"Kyle," Sheriff Drennan started as soon as Deputy Foster was seated, "are you feeling okay?" Sheriff Drennan's tone had changed from directive to inquisitive.

"Of course, I am," Deputy Foster responded. "Why would you ask?"

"Kyle, I have been out to visit Bill Anderson's farm today. I have a list of dates where he has filed trespassing complaints. I have searched our dispatch system and find almost none of these were ever entered. In addition, Anderson says you responded to nearly all of these complaints. How do you explain this?"

Deputy Foster slid a little deeper into his chair. A red blush began creeping up his neck and into his face. He tilted his head back and stared at the ceiling.

"Sheriff, it seems I haven't followed proper protocol. I truthfully didn't want to get into a lot of paperwork, when all I really needed to do was just show up and run off a bunch of kids partying in the cave."

Sheriff Drennan's gaze never left Deputy Foster's eyes. What was actually only a minute seemed like five minutes as the tension between the two started creeping upward quickly. It was finally broken when Sheriff Drennan leaned back and picked up the leave report Opal had created for him.

"Another interesting fact: I see you have taken a considerable number of vacation days over the past few years . . . and even more interesting, is that these days are the following days of the mysterious complaints."

With that last statement, Sheriff Drennan returned his harsh and directive glare toward Deputy Foster.

"Well, that must just be . . ." Deputy Foster began.

However, before he could complete his answer, Sheriff Drennan interrupted, "Kyle, I'm going to call the nurse in for a probable-cause drug test. I'm sure you understand the impact."

Deputy Foster sat in his chair staring back at Sheriff Drennan. His red face became almost crimson. The two sat staring at each other for a long, silent time.

Finally, Deputy Foster leaned forward and placed his head in his hands. In a timid voice he simply stated, "Don't bother; it will come out positive."

Sheriff Drennan placed the papers back on his desk and rubbed his face.

"Tell me this: were you stealing drugs from the kids in the caves?"

"No, not stealing. They *gave* me the drugs to keep quiet and not run them in," Kyle responded in a defeated voice as he continued slumping in his chair. "I guess I need to resign."

"Deputy Foster, I will not accept a resignation. You have committed a crime."

Sheriff Drennan stepped forward and opened the door in a jerking manner.

"Deputy Lane, please come here."

As Deputy Lane arrived in the doorway, Sheriff Drennan turned to Deputy Foster and requested his gun and badge. Deputy Foster complied as he stood up to face his direct report.

"Deputy Lane, please take Deputy Foster to a holding cell

and read him his rights. Then call the county prosecutor; I need to speak to her."

Deputies Lane and Foster left the office and headed toward the cell. Sheriff Drennan again returned to his chair and angrily swept the report to the floor with his arm. After a few minutes of simply staring off into space, he stood up, grabbed his hat, and decided to call it a night . . . again.

_____ Chapter 9

The next day was full of activity for Sheriff Drennan as he had to meet with the county prosecutor and answer a lot of questions from his staff. The day would be emotionally charged, and Sheriff Drennan did not like emotion.

He looked forward to escaping the office for lunch as he never got the chance to eat dinner the night before with Ashley. Just as he made his move to leave, a middle-aged woman approached Opal in front of him.

"Excuse me," the lady stated, "I would like to speak to the investigator covering the cave with the skeleton, please."

The lady was small, well dressed, and well-manicured. Opal looked up from her desk and then directly to Sheriff Drennan as he tried to pass by, hopefully, unnoticed.

"Of course. Sheriff, are you available?" Opal asked with an almost sarcastic flare.

Sheriff Drennan stopped mid-step and smiled with a defeated grin. Slightly nodding, he answered, "Of course." As he ushered the lady into his office, he added, "Please step into my office."

The lady followed his instructions and entered into his office. She sat in the guest chair with a suitably straight back and her ankles crossed. She was a proper belle who clearly had been to cotillion. The sheriff took his seat behind his desk.

"I'm sorry to bother you, Sheriff," she began, "but I felt compelled to visit. My name is Tonya Schmit. You see, my son, Jared, has been missing for almost five years now."

Sheriff Drennan could hear the tremble in her voice. She took a deep breath and regained her composure.

"We have been very blessed in our lives to live comfortably. My husband is a dentist in town. His father before him was also a dentist. Sadly, that comfortable living has afforded us things that it shouldn't have. Jared became heavily involved in drugs while in high school. He tried to commit suicide three times that I know about. Each time, we were able to rescue him. We had him in counseling, but he often ignored his appointments. Then he started regressing and wanting to party with his druggie friends. You see, his friends are likely some of those people who may be involved with the skeleton in the cave."

Upon hearing that, Sheriff Drennan's body language completely changed.

"Ma'am, how do you know about the skeleton?"

"Oh, news gets around fast here, Sheriff. But more importantly, I think you found my Jared. Jared was approximately six feet tall; and like I said, he's been missing for more than five years."

Sheriff Drennan didn't even look at his notes. He wasn't the investigator that measured the skeleton, but his guess would have been six feet tall.

"Sheriff, do you think that skeleton is my Jared?" the lady asked.

Her eyes were the eyes of a mother in pain. Sheriff Drennan admired her strength to approach him and have this very difficult conversation. He contemplated what to say next. He moved to the chair to sit next to her. Lowering his gaze, he stared at his hands.

"Ma'am, I think that's a strong likelihood. I'm very sorry."

The lady made a quick, small gasp, then replied, "No, it's better to know. When will you have a definite identification?"

"Soon. In fact, with this information, it may be quicker than we had expected. I'll make some calls."

The lady stood up, slightly wavering. The sheriff stood, as well, and offered a hand to steady her.

She looked at Sheriff Drennan and with composure and confidence said, "I'll leave my contact information with Opal. Please, do let me know the second you have something definite."

With that, she turned, head held high, and casually walked out of Sheriff Drennan's office toward Opal. Sheriff Drennan plopped into his chair.

"That's what this is all about: drugs. At least two lives ruined . . . one from suicide, another from greed."

With that, Sheriff Drennan made a few notes in a folder and tossed it on the pile behind his desk, believing the case was probably closed.

*****

Days passed and Jim found himself loading Jax up for yet another stream adventure. This time he would be monitoring land owned by the state of Arkansas to verify it was not being abused or that there were no squatting activities taking place.

Jim arrived in Siloam Springs and decided to step into a coffee shop for a little energy boost. Truth be known, Jim loved the frou-frou coffees . . . tough on his masculinity to admit it, but he loved sweet coffees with a little whipped cream.

Since the coffee house was a dog-friendly shop, he snapped the leash on Jax, which proved, yet again, to yield the disapproving Aussie head tilt. The duo stepped into the tiny, alluring, aroma-filled shop.

The coffee shop was a hybrid coffee shop-and-bookstore combo. Jim wasn't certain if patrons were allowed to read the books lining the walls or if the books were merely decoration. Regardless, the walls were covered with books. At the front of the shop was a small counter. One side of the counter was for ordering anything related to coffee; the other housed local pastries behind a glass dome.

The lady at the counter was busy helping others when Jim walked in. He decided to review the selection one more time in the event he had missed a worthy flavor. After taking some deep breaths, which his senses enjoyed, he realized Sheriff Drennan must have the same addiction as he had just purchased coffee and was walking toward the door.

"Hello, Professor . . . I mean, Mr. Cunningham," Sheriff Drennan spouted off as he arrived in close proximity. "How goes the world of fish?"

Jim, in a state of surprise as he didn't think Sheriff Drennan would remember him, was certainly unsure where the title "Professor" came from.

"All going well at the moment," Jim replied. "Just out checking some of the state land this way." Trying to keep the conversation alive, he continued, "By the way, have you heard anything about our little discovery last week?"

Sheriff Drennan took a long sip of what appeared to be much-needed coffee and replied, "You know, I haven't heard anything back from the crime lab; but I may know whose body that is. About five years ago, there was a kid from Siloam Springs who got caught up in behavior way over his head. He was probably a good kid from a respectable, wealthy home; but he started running with a crowd known for drugs. He may even have been trespassing on other people's property . . . likely a landowner named Bill Anderson. The parents searched and searched for years. I think his mother is still searching but ready for some degree of closure. She visited me just two days ago. She mentioned he had tried to commit suicide several times. I'm pretty certain that's whom we will identify."

Jim nodded his head as that seemed such a plausible explanation.

Sheriff Drennan continued, shaking his head as he added, "Likely a suicide."

At that moment, Jim's gaze was captured. A lady, who looked as though she could be the lady whom Jim saw sitting on the porch of the cottage, strolled by from the back of the coffee shop.

"Hello, Sheriff," she said in a confident, but definitely southern voice.

"Fine day to you, Kat," Sheriff Drennan replied as he tipped his hat.

She smiled at Sheriff Drennan then glanced toward Jim and smiled again as she continued her gait out the door.

The sight of the lady's eyes enthralled Jim. To say her eyes were blue was like saying a rose is red . . . sufficient, but certainly not accurate. Her eyes were blue like a lake or like a perfect raindrop. The expression of her eyes revealed narratives of her experiences. He thought to himself that the twinkle in those eyes was the most beautiful thing that a person could see in their short lifetime.

Jim was still gazing in her wake as she left the room when Sheriff Drennan chuckled, "Boy, don't get your hopes up there. Many men have tried to date her, but she doesn't seem interested. Hell, if I wasn't married to the meanest woman in Benton County, *I* would even give it a go."

Sheriff Drennan caught Jim off guard as he didn't know the sheriff had the capability to laugh. The sheriff slapped Jim on the back, reached down and petted Jax on the head, and proceeded out the door. Jim, regaining his purpose, purchased his coffee and loaded Jax back into the truck, headed to no-man's land.

Chapter 10

November arrived in rare form: beautiful, chilly mornings and cool days. Jim arrived in Little Rock to deliver a trout update to the Arkansas House of Representatives. He was early, which was good. He was never early anywhere he went. He thought Jax would have been proud of him in that moment had Jax been allowed to come with him.

He grabbed his computer bag, straightened his collar, and headed to the conference room at the state capitol. Suddenly, a moment of panic hit him.

"Now, where is that thumbdrive with the presentation?" he mumbled under his breath.

He did the usual pat down of his pants pockets and coat pockets. He looked through his computer bag. Yep, he did manage to remember his keys but had forgotten the thumbdrive. He quickly called his secretary, who was not shocked at his forgetfulness; and she started her exploration through his office. While still on the phone, she informed him that she had found the thumbdrive, so she would email him the presentation . . . so much for Jax being proud of him. (Jim decided to never speak of this to him.)

Another disaster narrowly averted, Jim decided to go to a nearby coffee shop—because it was not possible to have enough coffee—and await the rescuing email from his secretary. This coffee shop was distinctly different from his favorite one in Siloam Springs. This one was much more modern and contemporary. The counter was long and narrow. No pastries were to be found. At least three baristas worked behind the counter instead of one. The walls were sleek and gray. Historical black and white photos of downtown Little Rock plastered the walls. There were several small pods of comfortable chairs and mini sofas scattered around. Jim ordered his drink and found one of the few tables and chairs still available. Upon powering up his notebook, Jim heard a familiar voice.

"Mr. Cunningham?" the voice questioned. "Mr. Cunningham!" the voice repeated, more emphatically.

Jim glanced up over the top of his glasses to see the striking woman from the cave crime scene in October, only this time her dark hair was down, and she wore civilian clothes.

"Good morning, Detective . . ." he paused as he couldn't remember her name.

"Garringer," she replied so as to rescue him. "I saw you come in and thought I would say hello. I'm here for some professional development meetings," she continued.

After saying "professional development," they both rolled their eyes and chuckled. Jim invited the detective to join him. She gladly accepted and settled in with her grande coffee and took a sip. Jim admired her flexibility as he was certain he could count not less than six guns on her person.

"So, have you had any updates from Benton County?" Detective Garringer blurted out.

"It seems it was a suicide," Jim responded. "Sheriff Drennan—who, by the way, now refers to me as 'Professor' . . . and why? I do not know—suspects that a well-to-do kid from Siloam Springs overdosed in the cave on purpose."

Jim watched Detective Garringer's eyes narrow as she drank her coffee even more slowly than before. Jim noticed an awkward silence forming. Certain he said something wrong, he started fidgeting and asked if her coffee was okay.

Detective Garringer took a deep breath and, with incredible control and purpose, said, "The body's neck was broken. How could Sheriff Drennan assume overdose?"

Jim caught his breath as he couldn't believe what he was hearing. Just less than a week ago, Sheriff Drennan assured him that this was a tragedy caused by overindulging in a deadly recreation. Now, reality stated that this body had actually fallen victim to yet another form of tragedy. Not only was there the realization of the crime . . . but now, why?

Detective Garringer saw the puzzled look on Jim's face. She quickly divulged why she knew the cause.

"Mr. Cunningham . . . I mean *Professor*," she said with a grin, "I noticed when we were investigating the crime scene the significant injury to the cranium. It's what we refer to as a C3 break, the Hangman's Break. In addition, there was a quarter-sized hole in the back of the skull. This body clearly had at least a broken neck; most likely death was instantaneous. It's curious as to what weather event could have washed the body into that cave."

Jim looked even more puzzled than ever.

"Professor, I apologize that I haven't been much help on this case. You see, I was offered a promotion just a few days after we met at the crime scene. I passed the case on to my team to manage as I have been transitioning to a new role. To be blunt, I'm disappointed in my team for not contacting you."

Jim still sat, puzzled. Finally, he looked up into Detective Garringer's piercing eyes.

"There is no way that body could have had that significant of an injury and just end up in the attic of the cave. Detective Garringer, water could not have pushed a body into that crevice, because water never reaches that level of the cave. It had to have been placed there. We've watched the gauge results for that stream for the past 15 years, as we were and are certain that the cave protects a precious species of crayfish. Even during spring, that water level never rose more than three feet. The attic—or shelf—is at minimum seven and a half feet."

Detective Garringer's head started spinning. She was unaware of the sinister nature of Jim's finding until that very moment. Realizing that there was a clear oversight somewhere in this investigation, she assured Jim she would take a personal interest and would follow up with him. She stood up; and again, Jim was dazed at her striking height and fitness. She reached over and shook his hand, then headed out the door.

Jim sat awestruck. What started out as a quick moment to satisfy a caffeine addiction had suddenly turned into the strange feeling of insecurity, mystery, sadness, and conspiracy. He was awakened from his trance by his cell phone's vibrating. He looked at the caller ID and noticed it was his secretary.

"Why is she calling me?" Jim pondered.

Abruptly, he realized he was late for his meeting where he was presenting.

Chapter 11

Later that same day, Detective Garringer drove home via a route to David's Burgers, one of her guilty pleasures in downtown Little Rock. She loved the welcome she received each time she entered the restaurant. Today had been a long day, and it had been many hours since nourishment. She knew she had a workout the next morning, so how could this hurt? After gaining a quick whiff of fresh hamburgers and fries in her car, she headed home.

Home for Detective Garringer was a simple, but nice, one-bedroom apartment near the Riverwalk only minutes from her office. She stepped inside the door, hung her coat on the coatrack, set her backpack down on the floor next to the coatrack, and tossed her keys in a bowl on the foyer table.

The table only had three items on it: the bowl for keys and mail and two 8x11 framed pictures. One picture was of Detective Garringer wearing a Razorback uniform, crossing the finish line at a track meet; and the second photo was of her parents. Hung just above the table was a shadowbox housing one bronze Olympic medal for track and field. The medal caught her eye as it often did; and she gazed on it, almost as though she was gaining inspiration . . . or was it sadness?

She went into the kitchen and leaned against the kitchen counter as she dug the ever-coveted Dave's burger out of the sack. That night she didn't savor the flavor so much as devour it for energy sake.

She was still puzzled by the events of the day. She felt as though she needed to investigate a case that truly was not hers to investigate and one she was certain was going to come back to bite her in the butt.

Detective Garringer settled on her couch and pulled out her crime scene worksheet to verify some details. All crime scenes had a very particular set of details that she completed before returning the crime scene report to the local authorities. For instance, her report indicated "the temperature inside the cave had been measured at 58 degrees. Those present were Sheriff Drennan, Deputy Sheriff Homer Biggs, and Jim Cunningham. The body was found outside, yet in an inside, protected environment. The day of the discovery was crisp and clear at 69 degrees outside. The lighting inside the cave was dim to almost none. Preliminary survey of the scene: skeletal remains found on shelf of cave approximately 8 feet above the water stream. Most of the skeleton was intact; however, the femur could be seen in a different location close to ten feet away. The femur bone was broken into three pieces. The cave acted as a tomb and protected the body. Most of the clothing was intact, yet weathered from time: likely a blue, flannel-type shirt, jeans, and hiking boots. The boots were still recognizable as to brand and size. The soles had decomposed, but the laces and leather uppers were still in good shape. No jewelry was found. Visible break in C3 and hole in cranium. Jim Cunningham placed a 9-1-1 call; Deputy Biggs responded. No weapons found at the scene. No immediate suspects identified."

The report with her signature had been submitted four days after discovery. Notes had been made that all evidence was marked and photographed and the remains placed in appropriate paper sacks with identification and time stamp.

Detective Garringer logged into the iReports system under Company D, Northwest Arkansas. No preliminary findings were posted as of yet by the crime lab, but that wasn't really that unusual. Those reports were likely still a couple weeks out. Due to the fact that no immediate suspects were listed and that the crime had been committed most likely years earlier, the case would be declared low urgency.

She started thinking, "Now where to begin?" She laughed

as she continued thinking, "Why use state databases when the ugly truth can always be found on social media?"

Detective Garringer couldn't help but grin to herself as she Googled "Charles and Rebecca Moore." She selected the link to "Charles Moore, Kansas City." She discovered Charles had retired from G & L Trucking, a logistics firm that originated in 1962. It seemed he worked there for nearly 42 years. She found several pictures of his retirement party . . . delightful pictures of smiling faces. Many of his pictures had in them whom Detective Garringer supposed to be his wife. Rebecca appeared very proud.

Detective Garringer then searched Facebook. She noted that Rebecca had a very clumsy Facebook page that was full of pictures of young children certain to be Rebecca and Charles' grandchildren. Detective Garringer followed the timeline of the sale of their Kansas City home and the purchase of the "cabin of our dreams."

Detective Garringer then did a quick, criminal background search on both Charles and Rebecca Moore . . . no results. She propped her legs up on the ottoman and took a deep breath.

"These folks do not appear the criminal type," she half said to herself.

Her gut told her this was a crime that happened long ago . . . long before the Moores even considered the purchase of "the cabin of their dreams."

The purchase . . . who owned the property *before* the Moores? Detective Garringer quickly searched the property records only to discover Huck Ferguson was the prior owner. She felt a bit of a surge of energy. She heard the sheriff refer to Huck the day she bagged and tagged.

"Who was this Huck guy?" she thought to herself.

Again, the internet was such a good source for information. A simple Google search returned tremendous data. Huck was very active in the social and political scenes in Arkansas 15 years earlier. He was especially involved in fundraising campaigns for various Democratic leaders. It seemed if there was a photo opportunity, he was there.

Noticing how involved Huck was in the Democratic political circles, Detective Garringer decided to search the

Democratic fundraising reports since they were public information. She found Huck was an active contributor. She then decided to research all entities owned by Huck Ferguson.

She discovered Huck was the owner and operator of Ferguson Brokerage from 1988 to 2015 when his company was sold, as well as SP Industries from 1999 to 2015. The year 2015 was also the year the cabin was sold to the Moores. The deed to the cabin was signed by a Megan Ferguson, Power of Attorney. No death certificate for Huck Ferguson existed. Detective Garringer decided she needed to understand the relationship of Megan Ferguson to Huck and to the Moores.

Detective Garringer confirmed her suspicions that Huck was very charitable to many candidates, although Arkansas Governor Dobbs appeared to be his favorite. Huck seemed somewhat devoted to Governor Dobbs in his first bid for governor in 2010.

While perusing the reports, she noticed the location and sponsor of another consistent, well-known Democratic fundraiser, Sofia Agassi. Upon deeper searches, Detective Garringer discovered Sofia was an equal to Huck in many ways. She was an organizer of many large, politically-charged events. Sofia was also highly connected in the Democratic party, although she resided in Saint Louis, Missouri. In fact, Sofia was instrumental in the elections of the Missouri Governor Donaldson in 2009 and Senator Okeiff in 2007.

Huck and Sofia appeared at many events together. As Detective Garringer continued into hours of research, she finally landed on a very interesting set of pictures from an eager, middle-aged, mutual female friend of Huck's and Sofia's on Facebook. The number of selfies this lady posted was staggering. Detective Garringer shook her head at the obvious plea for attention this woman represented. She completely understood why the millennials moved away from Facebook to another app. Again, the exposure of people posting too much information on Facebook made Detective Garringer giggle.

There stood a young man and a young woman, Huck and Sofia, along with Governor Dobbs. It was easy to identify the folks as they were tagged. The young woman was Megan Ferguson who, she assumed, was Huck's daughter.

Detective Garringer couldn't help but follow the Facebook thread of Huck's and Megan's lives. They seemed so happy in so many pictures. Megan had a brilliant smile, was very attractive, and seemed to look at her father with adoration.

Detective Garringer could see how close they must have been. It occurred to her that there was no Mrs. Ferguson in the pictures. She quickly pulled up her Arkansas database and did a search for "Huck Ferguson." She found a marriage license for Huck Ferguson and Kerry Crabtree in 1982. Detective Garringer did another search for "Kerry Ferguson," only to discover a death certificate in 1996, "Cause of death: trauma as a result of a car wreck."

Now realizing that Huck and Megan were the entire family, Detective Garringer started researching "Megan Ferguson." She discovered that Megan was born in 1988 in Little Rock. She graduated from Pulaski Academy in 2006. Then Megan attended but never completed a fine arts program at the University of Arkansas from 2006-2009. Megan seemed to make the contribution circuit with her dad in 2009 and 2010. Then Megan seemed to go off grid, and she reemerged in 2014 in many different horror flicks—Megan seemed to have become an award-winning actress. She changed her name to Jacquelin Vanderli, which made the connection difficult to find.

Detective Garringer couldn't help but keep digging into more pictures and the well-to-do society of people posting them . . . pictures of happy Megan joking with Huck; pictures of Sofia working the crowd; pictures of Sofia's entourage clearly working and taking orders from Sofia; and a couple of pictures of stolen glances of young men looking at beautiful Megan.

This crime was unusual. She investigated many crimes in Little Rock. Most were premeditated murders or terrorist threats. This scene certainly fit the M.O. of previous crime scenes, though, with one exception: the people who were starting to be implicated.

She put the computer down and stretched out on the couch, laying her head back on a pillow. She just wanted to close her eyes for a moment. As she relaxed and her breathing slowed, the same thought kept streaming through her mind: what do all these people have in common, and what does any of this have to do with a murder in Cherokee City, Arkansas?

_____ Chapter 12

As Lori Garringer slept, her mind relaxed. Her dreams took her deep into her childhood. As a young Lori, she played in the overgrown yard. She could see her father and older brother loading cut trees into the holding yard of their sawmill.

It was only Lori and her brother now. Her older sister had died before Lori even met her. Her sister, Lilly, only lived three years. She had been born with a birth defect which caused water on the brain. Lori's mind flashed to a scene of her dad holding Lilly's baby picture at night after the work was done.

In her youth, Lori always felt conflicted. She could tell her dad loved her sister and never quite got over her death. She was uncertain, but it seemed he blamed himself somehow. Lori felt she was the replacement child. She never truly had her own identity growing up; she felt she shared it with Lilly. At times, her thoughts were vile toward the memory of Lilly. However, at other times, Lori was saddened that Lilly's life was cut short.

Lori dreamed of growing up trying to be everything to her father. He was a very tall Native American from the Cherokee and Iroquois tribes. He had a thin but muscular build.

Her dream quickly took her back to the sawmill. She worked alongside her brother, dressed in his hand-me-downs. She picked up the cut wood and loaded the trailer for her dad's customer, all the time watching her dad, hoping he saw how hard she worked. She wanted his attention and approval. Lori was a tad jealous of her brother: he was stronger, older, and seemed more in step with her father.

Lori dreamed of spending time with her mother in the evenings when the work was finished. Her mother was sweet. She always welcomed Lori to her with a smile and hug. Her mother had been quite strong in her younger years as she used to work at the sawmill with Lori's father. However, she seemed very weak these past few years. Her body was shrinking; she became easily winded when working. Her father tried to care for her and, at the same time, maintain an income. In Lori's dream, she continued to watch her father who, it was clear, was in emotional pain as he helped her mother to the bedroom every night, insisting she rest.

Lori's dream then turned dark, remembering the day her mother could not get up. She remembered the doctors and family visiting to pay their final respects. Her mother whispered to her that she was the light of her life. She smiled and told her daughter that some pigs have wings; they brought good luck. Her mother quickly faded away in a simple, worn, patchwork quilt-covered bed.

Lori's dream never fully regained delight again. She continued to remember the darkness of the days after her mother died. Her father started drinking. He drank to the point of losing control. He would anger easily. When he angered, he would strike her or her brother.

They both quickly learned to retreat into the yard or to the woods when the drinking started and return late in the night. The woods became her refuge. She found peace and solace in the trees and wildlife. She ran up and down the steep hills to get away from her father or to get back into the house before daylight. She often thought that was the beginning of her track career.

On days her father did not drink, he was still a kind and introverted man. That father, she often felt compassion and pity for. He soon moved on to dating and quickly remarried. Lori was stunned and overwhelmed that her father would even try to replace her mother so soon. However, he seemed happy and at peace.

Sadly, that peace faded quickly. Lori suffered from the hands of her new stepmother. She was quick to scold and never found anything to like in Lori or her brother. The stepmother often argued with their father as they experienced even more financial difficulties. The days full of dispute lasted more than 24 hours at a time.

Lori and her brother once again retreated into the woods. Lori's heart rate always seemed to slow down when she remembered the blissful, wooded retreat.

Her father and stepmother divorced after her stepmother decided the local grocer was a better-suited spouse. Again, her father drank.

And yet again, he remarried. The good fortune this time was that this stepmother was sweet . . . a kind and petite woman. Lori wanted a relationship with her; but still feeling the pain of losing her own, treasured mother and having survived emotional and verbal abuse from the first stepmother, Lori was standoffish. Soon Lori left for college on a scholarship and never returned.

Lori continued dreaming, wavering back and forth from her own memories to projected feelings that Huck's daughter, Megan, must have felt, as the dream mingled into one thread. Lori somehow felt drawn into Megan's mind.

Lori woke suddenly with a thought, "The young man! Who was the young man in Megan and Sofia's photos?"

Detective Garringer powered up her laptop. She noticed Megan with the young man from the original picture of Megan, Huck, Sofia, and Governor Dobbs. Since it was on Facebook, she found the young man tagged. His name was Dave Reid. Detective Garringer tried searching for Dave's social media footprint. She found almost nothing. It was like his profile existed, but nothing was populated . . . as if he had been partially erased.

She pulled Dave Reid's information up in her Arkansas Crime Information Center (ACIC) database. He appeared to her to be the bad-boy type . . . certainly there were some tickets warranted somehow. Nothing was found under his name in Arkansas.

It made sense to just Google him, as well. "Dave Reid" produced more than a few results, one of which was a hockey player in 1964. She could at least mark that one off the list, as Dave looked to be approximately 20-24 years old in the pictures with Megan. As she continued to scroll, none of them seemed to fit the young man in the photos.

Using that tidbit of information, Detective Garringer searched the National Crime Information Center (NCIC) database for "Dave Reid, male, Caucasian, 24 years old." What she read next completely reenergized her tired psyche: "David A. Reid, Columbia, Missouri, Missing Person."

Detective Garringer pulled up all the information from the Missing Person Report of November 2010: "Dave Reid, born in 1986, Columbia, MO, BA in Political Science, University of Missouri, 2008, employed at Sofia Agassi Consulting Services."

Detective Garringer sat on her couch with chills running down her arms.

"Sofia Agassi, how are you connected to all of this?" she whispered to herself.

Her gut told her the body belonged to David Reid. She would have to alert the crime lab to test the body's DNA against David Reid. But now the questions became more real, more tragic, more curious. If she was right, what was David Reid from Columbia, Missouri, doing in Cherokee City, Arkansas?

Detective Garringer looked up the address to Dave Reid's parent's home. She started planning a Saturday drive to St. Louis. She wasn't ready to reveal to her captain that she was delving into a cold case. Besides, it was midnight; and Detective Garringer knew she needed to get some sleep.

Chapter 13

Each day as Jim woke up, he wondered if it would be the day that he would hear back from Detective Garringer. In the days after their accidental meeting in the coffee shop, Jim had spent significant time remembering everything he had seen at the cave that day.

What had happened in that cave years ago? Why had he not heard or read anything in the news? The news was covered up with stories of college football fanatics and the pomp and circumstance leading up to the holidays. It seemed to him that a murder—despite it was eight-ish years old—would make headlines.

Jim managed to drive to the state Wildlife Office. It wasn't much of an office, more of a warehouse-looking facility with offices carved into the front. Boats, motors, nets, and equipment from the ark were all stored in the back in a haphazard, will-organize-any-day-now type of system.

Jim opened his emails only to read more bureaucratic hubbub from his chief. What was most amazing to him was how quickly people, who were dedicated to saving the environment, would turn into a true "politician" for a promotion. He read the emails with his chin resting in his hand.

"Fish need water, Moron," muttered Jim to himself, making certain his secretary could not decode.

His phone rang, an unknown number popping up on his caller ID.

"Hello, this is Jim," he answered, distracted by another email that landed into his inbox.

"Mr. Cunningham, this is Detective Garringer. Would you happen to have a few minutes to meet at the coffee shop on Main Street?" Detective Garringer very diplomatically queried.

"Of course. I can . . . uh, be there . . . yeah, I can be there in 15 minutes," Jim excitedly responded in a tongue-tied manner.

After having hung up, it occurred to Jim, "How did she get my cell number?"

Fifteen minutes later, Jim walked into the Main Street Coffee Shop. His senses were overwhelmed by his favorite fragrance: coffee! The coffee shop clerk waved to Jim warmly.

"Good morning, Jim," she said. "The usual?"

"Thanks, Valerie," Jim responded.

Jim peered over toward the corner of the store . . . of course, it would be the corner. There sat Detective Garringer, laptop opened. Seeing Jim, Detective Garringer motioned him over to her table. In fact, she already had a coffee for him. Jim was grateful as he guzzled a large sip, only to realize the coffee was just as he liked it.

"How does she know that?" he noted mentally.

"Mr. Cunningham, I have a few questions about the cave crime. Do you have some time to help me?" Detective Garringer opened the conversation.

Jim nodded his head as he took in another gulp of God's nectar.

"Mr. Cunningham, can you tell me about the layout of the skeleton when you found it?" Detective Garringer started.

"Of course. It was laid out the same as you found it . . . like a man lying on the ground. The skeleton was untouched by me or my team. Why? Did you gain any kind of information from the medical examiner?" Jim questioned.

"Yes, I did reach out to the examiner. The results are still pending as the examiner felt this is not a priority, but he did confirm the conditions of the bones did indicate a minimum of eight years' exposure," Detective Garringer revealed. "Do you, by chance, know the landowners?" Detective Garringer continued.

"Yes, I met the Moores a couple of months ago when I made my annual plea to explore their stream and land in search of the crayfish," Jim explained.

"Yes, but what do you know about the *previous* landowner, Huck Ferguson?" Detective Garringer pressed.

"Oh, Mr. Ferguson? That's different. I didn't know him well at all . . . never even met him. I understand he was a successful commodity broker. He denied my request to explore his land and stream for the last 15 years. I heard he had a stroke; and afterwards, his daughter actually sold the land to the Moores," Jim confessed.

After listening to Jim's response, Detective Garringer confided information to Jim in search of gaining his perspective.

"It seems she sold his company *and* his land. I didn't know about a stroke. But what is interesting to me is that he was also a major fundraiser for the governor. Governor Dobbs was campaigning for election in 2010. He was a strong Democratic candidate who won that same election."

Jim sat at the table continuing to enjoy his coffee. Finally sensing a pause in the conversation, he asked, "What does this have to do with the body?"

"I don't know. What I do know is that the body has been there, according to an uncorroborated opinion from the crime lab, for more than eight years. I know nobody has been allowed on that land for more than ten years. I know it was a homicide and not a suicide. What I don't know is why and who. I was hoping you had additional information."

At this point, Jim started to feel a bit concerned that he was being viewed more as a suspect rather than an eyewitness.

He shrugged his shoulders and responded defensively, "I have no other information, Detective Garringer. I'm just a biologist who is trying to improve the environment. I don't know these people . . . have *never* known these people."

Detective Garringer stared at Jim for what seemed five minutes. Then a calmness came over her.

"Mr. Cunningham, I apologize if I seemed to come across as accusatory. In fact, I am hopeful you have some insight as this case seems to be stifling. It is always difficult to solve cold cases."

"Of course." Jim realized the detective was merely searching for pieces of a puzzle and so softened his tone, "Please feel free to ask me *any* questions. I am glad to help."

"Thank you," Detective Garringer smiled in appreciation. "Mr. Cunningham . . . *Professor* . . . I feel like I have so much more research to do. I thank you for your time."

They both stood and Jim, being a southern gentleman, held the door for her.

"Please feel free to call me anytime. It seems you have my cell number," Jim smirked, hoping he had not pissed off the tall woman with a gun.

Chapter 14

After a long day at work, Detective Garringer returned to her apartment, placing her keys in her foyer bowl. She quickly glanced at her parents' picture in passing and plunked down on the sofa. She rubbed her face as though to stimulate thought through the pores of her skin.

She slowly sat up and grabbed a notepad from her coffee table. Scribbling on the notepad she wrote, "Huck Ferguson." She then drew an arrow to a stick figure body and wrote, "8 years (2010), Democratic Donor, Commodity Broker," and finally, "Megan." Detective Garringer stared at the paper trail.

"Where to begin?" she pondered. She circled "Democratic Donor" with confidence and headed to bed.

The next morning, Detective Garringer arrived at the Arkansas State Democratic Party Headquarters in Little Rock. She had called and requested a meeting with Executive Director Robert Quinn. Mr. Quinn came into the room all smiles and ready to entertain an Arkansas State Detective.

"Detective Garringer," he loudly professed through a mouthful of oversized, white teeth, "what brings you to our little part of the world?"

Detective Garringer, no stranger to working with the finest of Arkansas legislators, greeted Mr. Quinn with a smile and a handshake as Mr. Quinn moved to his desk chair and motioned for her to sit in an overstuffed guest chair.

"I am doing some research on a cold case from many years ago," Detective Garringer began.

Mr. Quinn was taken aback by the topic of conversation

and became somewhat uneasy by Detective Garringer's directness.

"I'm certain I cannot help you, Detective; but I'm happy to answer any questions you may have," Mr. Quinn defended himself, still grinning largely.

"Good!" she continued. "Do you recognize the name, Huck Ferguson?"

Mr. Quinn was stunned, becoming a bit nonresponsive for a second time in just a few minutes.

He stuttered as he responded, "Yes, as a matter of fact, I've known Huck for a couple of decades. He is a great guy. I first met him in something like 1994, when I worked for Carver Wealth Management Services. I worked there until 2006."

Detective Garringer continued, "Has Mr. Ferguson been a major campaign fundraiser for Governor Dobbs?"

"Why, yes," Mr. Quinn replied. "Yes, Mr. Ferguson has been a tremendous presence in our party for years . . . likely until his illness just a few years ago. Can you tell me why you are asking about Mr. Ferguson's contributions to the Democratic Party?"

"It is part of an ongoing investigation. Do you know if Mr. Ferguson had any enemies or had any conflicts?" Detective Garringer continued.

Mr. Quinn was clearly starting to feel uncomfortable about the conversation. He replied . . . but this time the grin was gone, and it was an all-business style Mr. Quinn who spoke.

"Huck was a great friend to everyone. He was generous to a fault. Obviously, in his line of business, I'm certain some people felt he made money off them and didn't share in his good fortune. But to be fair, that's how commodity trading works."

Detective Garringer stared Mr. Quinn down and subtly nodded her head.

"How close were Mr. Ferguson and Governor Dobbs?" she inquired.

Mr. Quinn moved from sitting behind his desk to stand and lean against it instead.

"Actually, I introduced them during the time I worked for Carver. Detective Garringer, I'm certain you understand the sensitivity of the questions you are asking about Huck and Governor Dobbs' relationship. If you cannot be transparent about why you are here and what you want from me, I fear I cannot continue this conversation," Mr. Quinn boldly and irritatingly responded.

"Certainly, Mr. Quinn," Detective Garringer answered directly. "I am investigating a murder of a John Doe eight years ago in Cherokee City. The body was found on Mr. Ferguson's land. I'm following the trail, as they say."

Mr. Quinn's attitude degraded even more from jovial during the welcome to slightly annoyed during the questioning to highly aggravated, which ended the inquisition.

"Thank you for stopping by, Detective," Mr. Quinn announced and held the door for her, hinting it was her time to leave.

She gathered her materials and walked into the main lobby. She left the headquarters, certain there was much more to Huck Ferguson than met the eye.

Chapter 15

Detective Garringer made the call to David Reid's parents and requested time with them the next Saturday. When Saturday arrived, she started her nearly six-hour drive to St. Louis. It was certainly a long drive, but Detective Garringer felt she needed to get some answers.

She arrived at the Reid's home a little after 3 p.m. A woman who, Detective Garringer was certain, was David's mother answered the door, a solemn look to her.

Detective Garringer introduced herself. "Mrs. Reid? I am Detective Garringer from the Arkansas State Police. I spoke to you on the phone the other day. May I come in?"

Mrs. Reid stood aside, inviting Detective Garringer into her home. She motioned to the sofa. Detective Garringer took her seat and very carefully began the conversation, as she knew this was an incredibly emotional moment for Mrs. Reid, regardless of the years that had passed.

Mrs. Reid weakly asked, "Have you found Dave?"

"No," Detective Garringer responded, noting she used "Dave" rather than "David." "In fact, I am following up on the Missing Person Report to see if I can help find answers for you. But sadly, no, I have not found Dave."

Mrs. Reid wore a strange expression on her face. It was almost one of relief but then followed by pain, which made sense to Detective Garringer and consistent with all the years and all the missing persons cases she had worked while on the force.

"Did Dave travel much into Arkansas while he worked for Ms. Agassi?" Detective Garringer asked.

As she spoke, she placed her elbows on her knees and leaned forward to show sympathy and respect to Mrs. Reid.

"Yes . . . well, I *think* he did," Mrs. Reid stumbled. "It has been so long ago. I don't remember Dave's travel details. He kept that to himself. He did seem to be always on the go . . . just the kind of life he wanted," Mrs. Reid continued.

"Do you think he and Ms. Agassi got along well?" Detective Garringer picked up and continued in a soft tone.

"Yes, of course. He did brag about landing a great job and being able to rub elbows with the elite and maybe someday the president," Mrs. Reid responded. "Ms. Agassi has been good to us. After we filed a Missing Person Report, she stayed in contact with us for many months . . . maybe even a year. She told us that we were welcome to most any information Dave might have kept at the office. She said she has never been more impressed with a young man as much as she was with Dave. You see, she recruited Dave out of college. He worked for her as an analyst . . . and she promoted him. Ms. Agassi said she really relied on Dave as he was so inquisitive and clever."

Mrs. Reid seemed to perk up while describing her son to Detective Garringer.

"He sounds like he was . . . is . . . a very talented young man," Detective Garringer mis-stepped in her questioning.

She could see Mrs. Reid was struggling with the interview.

"How painful this must be for a mother," Detective Garringer thought to herself. She glanced back up at Mrs. Reid as she continued, "Do you know if Dave had a girlfriend in the past?"

"Yes," Mrs. Reid quickly responded, "but I am unsure who she was. For some reason Dave kept that to himself . . . but I suspect his brother, Jeff, would know. Jeff is in the backyard working on my fence. It's just the two of us now," Mrs. Reid said, more as a somber thought than a statement. "I'll take you to him, if you like," she offered.

Detective Garringer agreed and followed Mrs. Reid outside to the back patio to meet her son, Jeff. They found Jeff tugging on an old wooden fence, clearly pulling out rotten boards to replace them. From the sound of the barking next door, Detective Garringer was pretty certain as to why.

Jeff was a tall, young man in his mid- to late-20s, making him the younger brother. A strong square jaw seemed to create a bit of an outdoorsman look.

"Jeff," Mrs. Reid said in her motherly tone, "this is Detective Garringer from Arkansas. She has a few questions for you."

Jeff very obediently dropped his tools and approached the porch.

"Have you found Dave?" Jeff immediately inquired, yet with some negativity in his voice.

"No, I have not; but I am following some leads from a cold case I am working on. I would like to ask you a couple of questions," Detective Garringer began.

Jeff nodded while reaching for a tissue he had stuffed in his pocket to wipe a drippy nose from the cold, December air. Mrs. Reid retreated back into the kitchen, leaving them both to converse.

"Do you know if Dave had a girlfriend?" Detective Garringer asked.

Jeff looked at her and then toward the kitchen. Detective Garringer picked up on a hesitation in his body language; so, she continued to push.

"Jeff, by chance was Dave dating Megan Ferguson?"

That seemed to catch Jeff's attention. She had clearly hit a nerve.

"So, you know about Megan, huh?" Jeff responded accusingly and very directly.

That was the confirmation Detective Garringer needed. At that moment, many more questions popped into her head.

"How long did Dave and Megan date?" Detective Garringer affirmingly asked.

"I don't know, to be honest," Jeff replied as he started to dig for gloves in his coat pocket. "I just know that Dave and I had drinks one night at a sports bar—maybe three weeks before he went missing—and he told me he was crazy about Megan. He was even thinking about proposing . . . but then he said not to tell anyone because there was something that he had to check out first. I have no idea what that was.

"At first, I thought maybe he thought she was seeing someone else on the side and he wanted to verify . . . but then . . . like his whole demeanor changed. He got all serious and dark. He said something about her dad. He told me that if Huck ever called that I should not answer and to keep an eye on Mom . . . sorta like 'keep her safe' kind of comment. I truly thought he was being melodramatic, because he can get that way . . . especially when he drinks."

As Detective Garringer watched Jeff respond, she could sense the intensity of the pain of loss in Jeff . . . and truly, frustration.

Jeff continued, "I tried to find Dave for months . . . almost a year. I called every friend I could think of. I even tried to reach out to Megan, but she never returned my calls. I dug through his computer at work . . . his notes. Nothing. My mom was able to gain access to Dave's bank records, because he listed her on his accounts. I couldn't find anything there, except he did seem to like to purchase knick-knacks everywhere he traveled . . . not sure what that was all about. I assumed they were gifts for Megan . . . but I came up empty.

"Detective Garringer, I pray you are able to end our pain here. We are prepared for what you find, I assure you. It's time for Mom and me to close this chapter of our lives."

Detective Garringer looked deeply into Jeff's eyes and saw exactly what he was saying. There was an emptiness that resided there. At that moment, she knew she had to help this family, regardless of who was implicated in the process.

Chapter 16

The brisk, but not frigid, air of December certainly diverted a lot of people from enjoying the scenic wonders of the Ozarks . . . but not Jim and Jax. In fact, this was perfect, as there wouldn't be people around. Again, Jim was an introvert; but Jax was a canine extrovert.

Today promised yet another adventure. Jim wanted to get drone footage of a couple of the streams he had already surveyed. Getting footage while the trees were bare of leaves certainly eased the job. Drones were yet another hobby for Jim. He enjoyed the view the drone could capture, Jim's way of soaring with the eagles.

Jim and Jax once again drove to Cherokee City. He drove past Huck's land and felt a twinge as he recalled his experience not two months ago. But in fact, this was one of the streams he needed to document as he was still certain the endangered species of crayfish abode there.

Jim parked at the edge of the road and opened the door for Jax. Jax bounded out as he knew this was going to be a day of hiking. He became puppy-like during these moments. He would jump on Jim as if to say, "Hurry up! Hurry up!" He scurried after every sound while Jim prepared for the hike. Jax enjoyed the cool days exceptionally, as well as the chance to go exploring.

Jim picked up his backpack containing the drone and a water bottle. He and Jax started traipsing up the rocky trail toward the bluff. He noticed this bluff when his team discovered the skeleton on their original crayfish hunt. He knew back then he had to climb it.

Jim discovered a second, small, somewhat overgrown trail along the way that branched off the trail he was following. Jim was certain others had discovered the beauty of the bluff, as they should.

Jax was certainly excited and playful. He ran ahead of Jim, stopping and turning sporadically to make certain Jim was following like a good boy. He would give the Aussie shame tilt and then sprint further.

Jax often found more interesting things to do and see than Jim did. At one point, Jax was on the scent of some type of small critter. He sniffed around a brush thicket and jumped from one side to the other. He dug ferociously on both sides. Sadly, no prey was found; so Jax gave up the hunt and bounded further up the trail. He seemed to never tire. In fact, Jax was gaining energy as the morning grew older. Somewhere along the way there was a small, natural spring that had not yet frozen over. Jax couldn't resist the urge: he jumped through it, splashing about. Jim watched and laughed at the romping pup.

"Maybe I should've been a dog," Jim thought to himself. "Maybe Jax thinks I am the dog."

Jim carefully navigated around the limestone trail. He savored the fragrance of the cedar trees, reminding him Christmas was only days away.

In just a few minutes, Jim was at the top of the trail. The beauty of this bluff took his breath away. There was something about standing on that bluff alone, except for his four-legged huntsman, that gave Jim an appreciation for the world before him. The fields were vast. The trees were tall. The eagles were majestic.

He set his backpack down next to a peculiar, Y-shaped tree. He dug his equipment out and plugged in the battery which, he was thankful, he remembered to charge the night before. He considered that a small victory.

Of course, while Jim was rigging his equipment, he managed to drop one of the propellers in the tall grass. He knelt down to pick it up. While rummaging through the grass, he found a tiny, metal box. The box was no more than the size of a fat business card holder. It was rusted shut. Jim believed the box to be an antique. It had small scrolls on top of the lid, somewhat indicating an air of sophistication. He stuck it in his pants' pocket, patted it for safekeeping, and finished assembling his drone. He decided he would pry the box open once he returned to the truck.

Jim powered up the drone and exchanged his sunglasses with reading glasses. Having detected another critter to chase, Jax bounded off back down the trail.

Jim hovered the drone downstream, the direction the stream would flow, while keeping the drone high in the air and zooming in on the crystal-clear water. As the stream flowed around the bend, Jim caught some movement off to the side. He zoomed out to see what it was, as this might be a great opportunity to see the illusive, Arkansas black bear about which he had heard so much but for which he could never gain any evidence.

Instead of spotting wildlife, Jim saw a man—no, *two* men—walking around the mouth of the cave where the skeleton had been found. Thinking it must be investigators, Jim's first instinct was to move on. He hesitated and decided to get a closer look. The two gentlemen did not appear to be wearing any official badges or identification or uniforms he recognized. That was a clear violation of protocol if this was official business.

Jim continued to spy on the two men. They were using what appeared to be a metal detector.

"Strange thing to have along a water's edge," Jim whispered as though they could hear him miles away.

Then he noticed each man had a side arm. The guns were not government-issue police or wildlife service weapons. In fact, Jim was a little jealous of the nice weaponry.

At that moment, one of the men looked up. Jim was certain they heard the humming sound of the drone.

"Shit!" Jim very loudly exclaimed to Jax . . . wherever he was.

Realizing he had been discovered and this could escalate, he reeled in the drone. Once the drone was back in his hands, he looked back toward the cave but was unable to see much beyond the bend . . . no movement. Jim decided the two men, likely uncouth treasure hunters, were trespassing on the Moores' land; he would stop in and tell the Moores on his way out.

Jim quickly disassembled the drone and carefully placed each valuable piece back into its appropriate spot in the backpack case. Hoisting the backpack over his back, Jim was ready to hike back to the truck . . . only, he was forgetting something: oh yeah, Jax!

"Jax, let's go," Jim commanded.

Out of the brush, Jax appeared, covered in hitchhiker burrs and a smile on his face.

"Ugh," Jim thought, "there's hours of brushing that bushy coat ahead of me."

Jim laughed to himself and gave Jax a couple of loud pats to the side.

_____ Chapter 17

Jim started walking down the trail, enjoying the hike. He stopped to look at a couple of deer rubs on some of the younger sapling trees.

"There's a big boy out here somewhere," Jim told Jax, although Jax was on alert as if there was something close by.

Jax started barking.

"Stop that, Jax," Jim scolded.

It was a bit unusual to hear Jax bark, but he continued to bark even after being reprimanded. With that second set of barks, Jim knelt down next to Jax to calm him. Jax was visibly upset. His eyes were narrowed and dark; his mouth produced a shallow, continuous growl. His front right leg arched in the up position; the remaining legs were taut and ready to pounce. Jim had never seen Jax like that before.

"The bear . . ." Jim whispered excitedly. "Do you sense the bear, Boy?"

Jim sat, quietly stroking Jax and intently listening. He heard what Jax had already been hearing: the brush rustling ahead of them. Jim reached for his gun, only to feel an empty holster.

"Good grief! I left the gun in the truck. What good am I as a concealed carry instructor if I can't even remember to carry my own concealed weapon?" Jim again whispered to Jax.

Jim decided he and Jax better move to the big rocks for safety and to get a better vantage point of the bear following them. As they started their hasty retreat, Jim heard the all-familiar sound of a rifle . . . like a strike of thunder. Next to him, a tree exploded into splinters. Jim ducked and grabbed Jax to prevent him from attacking the hunter.

"Come on, Jax," Jim shouted, "we gotta get outta here! Bears don't shoot guns!"

Jim started running back up the mountain through the trees to seek shelter. Jax was close at his heels. Another sound of thunder struck, and more trees exploded . . . that shot was closer. Jim realized that he and Jax were being hunted. Just as Jim started to climb the rocks, he heard a third shot, but this time the shot launched out of the wall of rocks and detonated near the origin of whoever was hunting him.

"Get up here!" a female voice commanded.

Jim, already shaken, wasted no time arguing or requesting identification. He and Jax climbed behind a wall of rocks only to come face-to-face with Kat, the lady from the porch . . . the lady from the coffee shop. Her long, blonde hair was pulled back into a pony tail protruding out of a black ball cap. But Jim recognized those eyes.

"Are you hurt?" Kat quickly asked while never taking her eyes off the general area from where Jim and Jax had come.

"No, I don't believe we are," Jim responded.

They both heard another shot. Kat started to reload her shotgun.

Jim reached up and offered to take the gun, saying, "If you will allow me?"

She handed him the gun and what was left of her ammunition. Jim quickly loaded the gun, stepped up for a view over the rocks, and quietly waited. Jim knew he needed a good shot. He also wanted to know who was shooting at him.

The trees rustled, and he heard two men speaking. Jim was unable to understand what they were saying; they were not speaking English. Kat, as well, peered safely through a break in the rocks while holding onto Jax.

The men exited the safety of the tree line, guns drawn. Jim took a deep breath as he recognized the guns. They belonged to the men at the cave this morning.

Wasting no more time, Jim quickly made two, very careful shots, hitting the ground directly in front of each man. They were both startled and hurriedly retreated into the woods.

Jim's heart pounded hard against his chest. He wasn't certain if it was because he was shooting at a human or because the humans had been shooting at him.

Jim quickly reloaded the shotgun and shot again. He and Kat sat quietly and listened. No more footsteps. Jim looked over to Jax. Jax's body language has relaxed . . . to the point that Jax was biting his fur trying to remove any burrs he could. Jim, feeling a bit safer, stepped down to where Kat had moved for safety.

"So, what's a pretty girl like you doing in a place like this?" Jim asked with a grin. "I don't think we have been formally introduced. I am Jim."

"Cunningham," Kat interrupted. "I met you in the coffee shop with Sheriff Drennan. I am Kat Allred. And as to what I am doing out here, it just so happens I like to hike," Kat said with a smirk. "I was out here hiking this trail, like many a Saturday morning, when I heard the gun shot. I climbed into the rocks and saw you running this way. I could see two people following you but couldn't see them well. What did you do to make those guys want to kill you?" she quizzed.

Jim laughed and shrugged his shoulders. "I dunno. I don't even know who those guys are. But I'm gonna find out!"

Kat got up carefully, still looking toward the edge of the woods.

"Well, we better get out of here in case they reload and come back," she suggested.

They both decided to start their journey back toward her house. It would be a fairly long walk as they took the longer route, but it was in the opposite direction of the shooters.

Jim, starting to get his senses back from the adrenaline rush, asked Kat, "Why are you carrying a 20-gauge shotgun?"

Kat's smile lit up, which caught Jim's eye. "You see, I had a sweet, little dog until about six months ago. The coyotes attacked her and mangled her poor little body so much I had no choice but have the vet put her down. I decided at that point to hunt the coyotes like they hunted her."

Jim listened to her explanation and grinned. Not many people hunt coyotes consistently in this area. Most hunt deer.

But standing next to him was a woman seeking vengeance for her pet . . . respect!

"Have you killed any?" Jim inquired.

"Depends," Kat responded.

Jim's eyes narrowed as he shook his head in confusion.

"Depends if you are asking as Mr. Cunningham, who I met at the coffee shop with Sheriff Drennan, or if you are an official of the Wildlife Service," Kat continued with a crooked grin and a wink.

That was all the answer Jim needed.

Chapter 18

Jim followed Kat back to her cottage-style home. Unbeknownst to Kat, Jim constantly monitored Jax for any indication they were being followed. Jax revealed nothing alerting during their walk back, which Jim found comforting. He quickly studied the area around Kat's house one more time to make certain he could leave her in safety.

Kat opened the back door and invited Jim in as she carried her gun to her bedroom, Jim assumed, as she disappeared down the hall. Jim slipped off his boots and placed them next to the door. Jax rapidly bounced into the kitchen and immediately began exploring.

Her kitchen had a country, rustic motif. The countertops were solid gray and sparkling clean . . . a very modern look for a little house sitting in the country.

Jax circled the warm floor directly in front of the stove blowers. Upon the third circle, he collapsed his body down, crossed his two front paws, and laid his head snuggly on top. He gazed at the humans under slightly closed eyelids, always keeping guard.

In the corner of Kat's kitchen sat a small office desk with a computer and a comfy desk chair. Papers were stacked high but neatly. Her laptop was powered on as if she had been using it earlier that morning.

Jim dug out his cell phone and connected to Kat's Wi-Fi, cleverly enough named "PromisedLan." He dialed Benton County Sheriff Department and asked to speak to Sheriff Drennan.

"Drennan," the voice on the other end answered bluntly.

"This is Jim Cunningham," Jim started.

Before Jim could continue, Sheriff Drennan interrupted him by saying, "Good God, you didn't find another body, did you, Professor?"

Jim chuckled as he said, "No, I did not. But I almost *became* the dead body. Two men were creeping around the cave today. I guess they saw Jax and me as later they shot at all three of us."

"Three of us?" Sheriff Drennan repeated.

"Yes. Kat rescued me from becoming a trophy to hang on someone's wall today."

"What the hell was she doing out there?" Sheriff Drennan continued.

"She was hunting . . . uh . . . *hiking*," Jim stammered. "Anyway, I don't want those goons to hurt her."

"Ok, I'll send the patrol out. I think I may even pay her a visit myself," Sheriff Drennan continued.

Jim wasn't comforted by that last statement; however, the good news was that the police would be checking on Kat regularly.

Kat returned to the kitchen unarmed.

"So, Mr. Cunningham, tell me about yourself," Kat prompted in passing as she stepped to the refrigerator and grabbed a pitcher of sweet tea.

As she began pouring glasses of tea for Jim and herself, Jim started telling her the "Story of Jim."

"Well," Jim stuttered, "first of all, please call me Jim. I am a biologist for the Arkansas Fish and Wildlife Service . . . been doing that for 30 years. I am recently divorced. Jax and I live on Beaver Lake. I like coconut cream pie. And I'm on a traveling cornhole team."

Kat, who was looking into her tea glass, perked up at the last comment with a confused look on her face.

"Well, maybe I just like cornhole, but not really on a traveling team. I said that for your benefit," Jim replied with a smirk.

Kat's smile yet again lit up. She couldn't help but giggle at Jim's version of his life.

She replied, "I think you left out bones collector."

Again, Kat shot a smile toward Jim.

Jim, enjoying the banter, continued, "Well, if I told you everything I know, I would have to kill you." Before she could respond, he lobbed back, "And now that you know everything that is important about me, tell me about Kat."

Kat's eyes caught Jim's for a brief moment before she took a deep breath and replied, "Fair is fair. I am the marketing manager for Nations Bank. I've been doing that for about 15 years. I am widowed . . . have been for almost 12 years now. I have two sons. The oldest is a pilot for the Navy. The youngest has just started a job in D.C. for the State Department as an analyst. They will both be home for Christmas . . . I hope! And I am a Queen Bee!"

Jim's back stiffened when he heard the last statement.

"I'm sure you are" he uttered while snapping his fingers in a "there-ya-go" style.

Kat couldn't help but giggle again, "I am a beekeeper. I know it is kind of a strange hobby, but my grandfather taught me years ago; and I've continued his bee genetics, if you will."

"Oh," Jim nodded, "so, can I have some honey?"

Even Jim was embarrassed at how corny that sounded and covered his face with his cap while laughing to himself. Kat responded in laughs, as well. They both realized to themselves that they had faced a bit of danger; and now, less than two hours later, they were laughing together over sweet tea.

As Jim sat in the kitchen, he could see into the living room. Kat caught him gazing into the room and walked over to him.

"Come in and take a seat while you are waiting for Sheriff Drennan or his posse to arrive to protect me . . . yes, I heard you call him."

Jim happily obliged. As they moved into the living room, Jim could see many pictures of the two boys he was certain were her sons. A very large, rather recent picture of a strong, tall and thin, young man standing in dress whites hung on the wall. Next to it was an equal-sized frame of yet another, strong, tall, young man in graduation robes. There was no doubt who the men were in this lady's life.

Jim couldn't help but get lost in Kat's rather eclectic decorating style. The kitchen was rustic and somewhat sparse in decoration . . . very contemporary. But the living room was full of adobe vases, ceramic cats, woven baskets, little statues, and more. Kat noticed his glancing around the room.

"Before you ask . . . no, I am not a world traveler. One of my neighbors' old boyfriends used to bring me little trinkets from the many places he traveled. I think he felt I was a bit of a surrogate parent to him."

Jim watched Kat talk about the young man. He watched her transform into a somewhat melancholy mode. She examined each piece as though each knick-knack possessed some kind of history.

"So, which neighbor was that?" Jim questioned, hoping to change the mood.

"Aha . . . that would be Huck Ferguson," Kat replied, smiling as though she had been caught in a downhearted mood. "Huck was a good neighbor, although I didn't interact much with him. His daughter, Megan, is really more of my connection. You see, her mother died when she was very young . . . I believe when Megan was only seven or eight years old. Huck was a very busy professional. He was working in some type of commodity trading. They lived in Little Rock somewhere but spent most weekends here. I think Huck used his cabin as a bit of a retreat from the world so he could heal after his wife died in the car wreck. Megan was young and impressionable. She missed her mother so very much," Kat replied, as though she was reliving her experiences with Megan and Huck.

"Megan would often go for hikes. In fact, that's how we met: I found her on a trail years ago. Come to think of it, it was the same trail as the one you and I were on today."

Jim smiled, realizing that Kat clearly had a fondness for this little girl. He found the depiction of her memory mesmerizing. She lit up as she spoke about her neighbors. Jim was glad to know that Huck was a good man and a good neighbor to her . . . especially after finding bones on his former property.

"As Megan grew up, she and my boys were good friends. But honestly, she needed a female influence," Megan continued. "We included her in as many functions as we could. She is family."

96

"Do you still see her?" Jim asked.

"Almost never but, fortunately, in a couple of weeks she may come in for the holidays," Kat explained and again dropped her head into her chest and started fiddling with a small ceramic cat she had picked up from the shelf.

"You see, Megan grew up in such a way she was always seeking Huck's approval and love. Huck was busy. He just didn't give her much time. So, she tried harder and harder to get his attention. Then she met a boy . . . as they always do. She was probably around 19 or 20 by then . . . young. She was crazy about the boy. He had made quite the impression on one of Huck's acquaintances in Missouri. Honestly, I think he was brilliant," Kat continued, describing what was certainly going to end badly.

Laughing as she stared at the little ceramic cat in her hand, she looked up at Jim and smiled the saddest smile Jim thought he had ever seen.

"The boy was the one who used to bring me these little knick-knacks."

Jim sensed her use of past tense.

"Where is the boy now?" Jim inquired.

"He disappeared many years ago. It truly is the strangest thing," Kat replied with a puzzled gaze. "You see, he came by early one morning. He had just returned from the Sahara . . . I think Morocco. He brought me that silly little terra cotta vase sitting on that table. He was so happy.

"I believe his happiness was because he was in love with Megan and was going to ask her to marry him . . . something like that anyway. He showed me a little pill box. He kept saying he had something to give to Megan. Knowing him, he had found some kind of strange jewel on his travels and wanted to give it to her. They, too, had found the trail we both enjoyed today. I believe the bluff became their sanctuary.

"You see, Huck and Dave, the boy, had had some kind of falling out . . . a rather big blow up after one of Huck's fundraising events in Little Rock maybe two or three months prior. Huck came back to Megan the next day and forbade her to see Dave ever again. Huck said the boy was trouble . . . was a gold digger. I just can't imagine that.

"Anyway, I'm sure you can imagine the heartbreak for the poor girl. I tried to comfort her, but she was sick over it. That's why they started seeing each other secretly on the trail when Megan and Huck were here at their cabin."

_____ Chapter 19

"Anyway, I digress," Kat started again after a short pause. "The boy drove away from my house, which was odd. I assumed he was going to the bluff, but I guess he had other plans. Megan came by later and said she got a message from Dave to meet him at the bluff. She hiked up there to see him, but he never showed up. She tried calling him but could never reach him. Megan thought he got caught up with work and would call the next day. That happened often—especially in the last few months—so we weren't overly alarmed. He seemed to be doing a lot of traveling and research.

"After a couple more days, Megan got worried and reported it to the police. There was a lot of activity then, but the police said Dave had been seen by his employer just two days prior and had flown to Morocco on business. That was confirmed by the airline.

"Megan was still unable to reach him. Even his family had trouble locating him. In fact, since his trip to Morocco, nobody has seen or heard from him. The people from his work couldn't reach him. The police tracked him through immigration for years, and it never showed that he ever reentered the United States."

Kat became very serious. "Jim, honestly, I think Dave went to Huck that day to try to work things out. You see, Dave was a very traditional young man. He was clearly in love with Megan. I think he wanted to clear the air with Huck before asking Megan to marry him. Part of me wonders if Huck found a way to send the boy to Morocco where he likely met with trouble. I do believe Huck has somewhat of a sinister side even if he has been good to me."

Jim sat on the couch, watching and listening to Kat. Her story was taking a bit of a turn. What started out as a bit of flirtation on his end had resulted in a sobering moment.

He couldn't help but sit there and ponder, "Could Huck have killed Dave and drug him into the cave? But Dave's work confirmed he was in Morocco. Morocco? How do these pieces fit into the puzzle?"

Jim decided these were conversations best to have with Sheriff Drennan or Detective Garringer.

"Kat, you have been a great hostess, but I am a fish guy. I know when it is the right time to leave . . . before I start smelling," Jim said with a corny chuckle. "I'm gonna head back to my truck and I'll call Drennan on the way and let you know what he says."

Kat and Jim headed to the back door of the kitchen to grab his shoes.

"Your truck is a little walk. I'll give you a ride in my side-by-side," she said.

As Jim started to protest, Kat held up her index finger, "And don't argue with me."

Both smiled as Jim slipped on his shoes and started walking toward the ATV. Kat stopped and grinned at Jim. He caught her grin and smiled back, not knowing what else to do.

"Did you forget something?" Kat teased.

Jim went through the forget-me-not pat down procedure. Phone? Check. Keys? Check. Drone? Check.

"I seem to have everything," Jim replied, confused.

Kat grinned again while shaking her head.

"Come on, Jax," Kat commanded as she reached back and opened the door.

Jax leaped up from a deep sleep by the fire and ran out the door in front of them, almost as if to say, "What took you so long?"

Kat drove Jim down the road to where his truck was parked. He thanked Kat and started unloading his gear from the side-by-side into the back of his truck. As he leaned into the side-by-side to grab the backpack that housed the drone, he felt his pocket hit the side of the vehicle. He remembered the little box. He reached in and pulled it out. It was tiny and rusted.

He jokingly held up the box to Kat and said, "Hey, I'm leaving with treasure, so it was all worth it."

He chuckled as he held the tiny box, believing himself quite charming. Jim glanced over to catch Kat's eyes once more before calling it a day. He saw a stricken woman. Her face was white as a sheet.

"May I see that?" Kat asked.

"Certainly," he responded.

Kat picked up the box from his hand. She turned it from side to side while examining it.

With a tear perched on the edge of her lower eyelid, she looked up at Jim and asked, "Can you pry this open for me?"

"Certainly," he answered in a quiet tone, watching Kat very carefully with concern for her.

Jim reached into his truck and pulled out a screwdriver. After knocking off the rust, he was able to probe the screwdriver into the opening and pop it open. To his amazement sat a ring completely enthroned by velvet . . . but not just any ring; this ring was delicate, made of yellow gold, and revealed six prongs holding a single, large diamond that glistened in the sunlight.

Without saying a word, Jim, thinking that maybe Kat had lost such a ring because she seemed so emotional when she saw the box, simply handed the box to her with the ring still intact. Kat took the box from Jim and slowly picked up the ring out of the velvet pillow on which it rested, holding it up to her eyes which were now full of tears.

She looked over to Jim and with a cracked voice said, "This is the box Dave had with him when he said he had something to give to Megan. Where did you find this?"

Jim found himself dumbfounded. He knew what this meant and knew instinctively that Kat was going to know when he answered.

"I found it at the bluff this morning."

He watched Kat's eyes as they betrayed her every second. Her eyes told stories. Her eyes that he normally found so arousing now displayed terror and anger. Not knowing what to say, Jim stood in silence.

"Dave *did* go to the bluff. Dave had to have met with trouble. Dave didn't go to Morocco, did he?" Kat was reciting more than questioning. "That is Dave's body you found."

Jim could see Kat was in pain, but he had to agree with her.

"There is something wrong with that story about Dave and Morocco," he voiced their thoughts.

Jim carefully reached over and hugged Kat. He wanted to reassure her and not frighten her. His arms swallowed her. She melted into his chest and breathed deeply.

"Don't worry, Kat. I know someone who can help. Will you be okay here by yourself?"

Kat pulled back, appearing stronger. She looked up into Jim's eyes and nodded.

"I will be fine; nobody saw me. And thank you for helping me find out what is going on. Please keep me in the loop of whatever you find," she said with confidence. "I wonder if I should reach out to my son," Kat continued, almost in a daze.

"Please *do* let your boys know of what is going on," Jim subtly insisted. "They need to know, and we should all start checking in on each other daily."

Kat nodded, but Jim wasn't completely certain she heard him. He moved closer to her face and repeated, "Let's check in on each other daily, for safety sake . . . not just because I want to talk to you every day."

Jim smiled as, again, he thought himself charming. With that, Kat giggled and nodded.

Jim loaded Jax into the truck and headed back home. Once he was within cell range, he decided it was time to dial a friend.

"Detective Garringer," responded the voice on the other end.

_Chapter 20

Tory started another day in the western Sahara. The days were hot and humid even though it was December. She stared out across the strange mix of land that rested within her eyesight. Most of the landscape was inhabited by a vegetative state; yet sandy, loamy soil seemed to persist in places. She longed for the days of playing in the fields around Omaha. She missed the green, wavy stalks of corn. She missed the cool mist of rain falling on her face. She missed her family most of all.

Tory took another deep breath. The air was harder to breathe here. Her lungs felt as though they were full of dust. As her mind meandered through her druthers, she felt a tug on her pants leg. She stared down into the most beautiful, large brown eyes one could ever see. A small boy from the local tribe in Morocco was smiling at her, motioning for her to come with him. His smile seemed to encompass his whole face. His cheeks were drawn in. His wispy hair was almost non-existent. His bony fingers tugged and pointed.

"Good morning, Diwan," Tory teased back. "Are you wanting me to play?"

Diwan nodded and jogged forward.

Tory smiled at Diwan's playfulness. He was thin as a rail, but ready to play like any other child. A brutal future lay ahead for Diwan. He was born into a poor family. His father was allegedly convicted of theft and now worked in the mines. Diwan's mother had yielded to a future without a husband. Her three children suffered as she was the sole provider for them. They had very little food. They had no education. They had no medical care, except what Tory, a nurse, and the World Health Organization (WHO) provided.

Tory stepped back. She looked around the sandy desert and this time saw her purpose. This land was a forgotten land, but a land full of prospects and great futures . . . the future of every soul she saw and touched. She could see Diwan's future. She realized she was standing in the most beautiful place on Earth.

Tory laughed as Diwan played some version of tag with his younger siblings. She sat down in her small medical office and pulled up information on her laptop. She had to travel into town to connect and download information; regardless, she tried to write as much as she could while in her office.

She thumbed through several old, downloaded emails, one of which continued to catch her eye. It simply read:

"*March 2, 2010*
Ms. Tory Hamilton,
Pleased to meet you via halfway across the world. My name is Dave Reid. I work for many potential Congress hopefuls in the United States. I received your contact info from a Congressional representative who supports many of the fundraising efforts for WHO.

An issue has come up, which is near and dear to my heart: the human rights element in Morocco. I have limited information and education regarding anything concerning the Sahara. In fact, I have made two trips to your area in the last year and have one coming up in May.

I would like to meet you and would like to research a few things specific to the phosphate mines. Can you give me some information or contacts you would recommend regarding how the mines are managed?
Sincerely,
Dave Reid"

Tory remembered how excited she was to have someone who had heard her plea. She had worked hard to position

Morocco as a land in need. It seemed there were parts of the territory that were just too political to enlist help. She stood there watching Diwan play and thought about her childhood. Everyone deserved that opportunity. She had been here almost nine years now, and that was the best lead she had. She had hoped that Mr. Reid would have been more help in her plight.

Tory glanced back at the computer to continue to read her older emails.

"March 22, 2010
Mr. Reid,

A pleasure to virtually meet you, as well.

I can give you a synopsis and would be more than happy to meet with you in May when you arrive. Please forward me your travel details. I would suggest meeting at a small café in Sidi Tiznet, Hennah Café. Would be easy to meet there.

Phosphate mines are prevalent in Morocco. The land is in constant dispute as the rebels from the Polisario Front continue to create much disturbance and violence. The Polisario Front and Moroccan State Agency have been fighting for the last decade over the rights to the phosphate mines.

You see, phosphate is a very lucrative business. It is one of the few businesses here. Phosphate is demanded from the power countries, such as China, the United States, and India. Phosphate is processed into phosphorus, which is used in agriculture as fertilizer. Apparently, these larger countries have depleted—or nearly depleted—their natural resources. Therefore, they buy everything that Morocco can produce.

But sadly, that is the problem. The mines are owned by the Moroccan state. They use prisoners as workers. The WHO is not allowed in, which is troublesome as many folks on the perimeter of the mines are developing leukemia, brain tumors, and birth defects—all through reckless mining practices. It's like medieval times here.
Sincerely,
Tory Hamilton"

"*May 5, 2010*
Ms. Hamilton,

I plan to arrive in Morocco next Wednesday. I will forward more of my travel details. Hopefully, we can meet. I would like to see the things you are experiencing. As you know, many of the U.S. dollars are tied up in purchasing phosphate for agricultural use. As part of our Department of Labor actions, we, the U.S., are to monitor the compliance of the Tariff Acts that prevent purchase of goods obtained from use of prison labor. With all that said, I am also very concerned about the information regarding the conditions folks are experiencing. To be transparent, I don't know that I can make a difference, but I want to know more.
Sincerely,
Dave Reid"

_____ Chapter 21

Tory, hearing a loud noise, quickly moved to the window to see that Diwan had taken a spill outside of her office. He jumped up and again was laughing and running with his friends, apparently unharmed. Tory smiled as she watched the little boy play. She grabbed a cup of coffee that was sitting on the counter and walked slowly back to her desk. She took a sip, then dove back into reminiscing.

After reading those first emails, she remembered back to Dave's visit. Dave was a man of his word. He had showed up at the café Tory suggested in town. Tory remembered walking him through the village.

"This is a rural village, so the poverty here is significant," Tory had explained to Dave.

She watched as Dave took in the scenery.

"Be sure to keep a watchful eye out for the young ones as I take you to the mines. They will likely be fascinated by your presence. The mines are only about a 20-minute drive from here. Note that I cannot get you *into* the mines; I'm not allowed on that property. However, I can get you to the perimeter," Tory had told him.

Dave had nodded in confirmation that that was the best next step. He continued to take in the sights as he peered through the window of the vehicle in which they were traveling.

As she drove Dave that day to her office, which was facing the mines, she could see Dave's expression change from one of interest to one of concern.

He would frequently ask questions such as, "What goods are produced in the village besides phosphate?"

Tory had replied, "Wheat . . . on the right land they can produce lots and lots of wheat. But the villagers don't own the land. The lucky ones are employed by the larger landowners. They seem to fare okay."

Dave had nodded with understanding. Then he caught a glimpse of the even more poverty-stricken areas. The houses were mere huts. Many of the people who could not work were sitting on their stoops. They were thin. They were in despair. Dave looked at Tory; no words were uttered. Tory nodded her head. They both understood the devastation now.

Tory had pulled up to her office, feeble as it was. She invited Dave in to see what resources she had. Her patient care facility consisted of two large beds and a table for examination; a small cabinet of instruments; an even smaller, locked cabinet marked pharmacy; and a tiny, metal desk stacked with paper situated next to the window, which was the main source of light.

"It's not much, I know. But this is all these folks have. I do the best I can to be proactive in their care, as well as offer compassion to those for whom I know I can do nothing," Tory had declared. "But you came to see the mines, so let's step outside," she had continued.

Tory escorted Dave around the side of the little office. There, facing both of them, in the distance was the commotion of many trucks driving to and from a mountain. From what Dave could see, there was a clearly defined building where people in uniform were working.

"What you don't see is what is on the *other* side of that mountain," Tory had suggested. "The mine where they use prison labor is strictly prohibited and monitored. I can take you to a stoop where you can get a glimpse of it."

"I want to see it," Dave had sublimely responded, never lessoning his gaze.

Tory grabbed a canister of water and instructed Dave to follow. She gave him a head wrap as the desert sand would be a nuisance. Dave and Tory strolled through the end of the tiny village. As she passed people, many would recognize her and speak. Tory would stop by each one who reached out to her and check their heads for fever or quickly tend to a wound or even give instruction. Dave was amazed at the care Tory issued. The true look of heartbreak was noticed on her face.

"You really care about this village, don't you?" he had asked.

Tory stopped in her step and looked directly into Dave's eyes. "They are my brothers and sisters, my mothers and fathers, my nieces and nephews, my children and grandchildren. Their pain is my pain. And I fully intend to help as many as possible during my days on Earth," Tory very directly and unapologetically had responded.

Dave smiled as he had encountered true strength in Tory. Tory was a force to be reckoned with, all bundled in a petite, non-threatening, yet passionate, might.

Tory had turned and continued to a small hill. Soon, Dave and Tory were climbing. It was very lightly wooded and scattered with Step, a small bush in the Sahara. Step was known for its nutrient value for livestock, yet no livestock was present.

Tory reached the top and had instructed Dave to take a bit of cover behind a small formation of rocks. Dave then saw to what Tory was referencing. This second mine was nothing like the first. Men in tattered clothes were pulling phosphate out of the mine and loading giant trucks. The workers looked malnourished.

This was all Dave needed to see. Tory had seen the confirmation on Dave's face. They then retreated back to her office, and she later had driven him back to his hotel in town.

Tory remembered that trip back to the hotel with Dave. It was quiet. Neither of them spoke. She felt Dave would certainly help her find help for the villagers.

Tory's memory was interrupted by an old, tattered ball rolling through her office door.

"Miss Toreeee. Can you kick?" Diwan uttered, smiling his giant, perfect smile.

Tory arose from her computer, chuckled, and grabbed the ball out from under her table.

"Here ya go, Diwan, I'll be out later to play with you," Tory responded.

She watched Diwan exit the office and run as fast as he could to his friends. He chattered something and laughed. Again, Tory was pleased the children here could be children. She smiled as she watched Diwan disappear through the village.

Once again, Tory returned to her desk, sipped her coffee, and reminisced . . . but this time, she pulled up more emails from Dave.

"September 20, 2010
Tory,

Good morning to you there. I hope you received my little package of children's books for the village and beef jerky for you.

I need your assistance. Do you recognize any of these men? I found this picture in a file from a fundraising event. I am researching some connections.

Those whom I know are: (starting at the left) Arkansas Secretary of Agriculture Toby Dobbs; Huck Ferguson; Graham Barnes, the comptroller general of the U.S. Government of Accountability Office; and two men I do not know.
Enjoy that jerky!
Dave"

Tory replied to the email a few days later, affirming the identity of the men . . . and more.

"October 1, 2010
Good evening to you, Dave,

I did receive your care package. Thank you very much. Sadly, the jerky was more popular with the little boys in the village than the books. So, please send more. Ha!

Yes, I do recognize a couple of the men. I have never met these folks personally, but one of the men is, indeed, the Director of the Mines, Bin Moussa.

I also recognize the man you refer to as Graham and others. I am told he is a U.S. government official. He has been here many times. I have made many efforts to meet with him, as I have hoped he could help with the conditions of the mines, which would benefit the laborers. As you would guess, I have been unsuccessful. The mine managers don't seem to be impressed with my dazzling personality.
Tory
P.S. Again, please send more jerky!"

That was the last correspondence she had with Mr. Reid. She had such a good feeling about Dave, that he would be the connection to help her to help them. Tory stared out at the village in a bit of a daydream, thinking that was eight years ago . . . and her last solid hope.

She was shaken back to reality when a young mother appeared, standing in her doorway with a screaming toddler. Playing with Diwan was going to have to wait.

Chapter 22

Graham Barnes, comptroller general for the U.S. Government Accountability Office, leisurely walked into his office holding a Starbucks cup in one hand and a wool coat draped over the other hand. His secretary, Nathan, welcomed him and reminded him of a morning meeting with the Majority Whip.

Graham nodded and grinned, "Of course, of course."

Graham sat down in his chair and started making his morning calls. His calls were more of a "good ol' boy" roll call.

"Kevin, how was dinner with the Appropriations people last night?" Then in an outburst, Graham guffawed and said something like, "She could start an argument in an empty house," or "Don't piss on my leg and tell me it's rainin'."

Graham was the master charmer. He was from Virginia and proud of it. His southern accent and sayings were highly acclaimed on The Hill. He introduced himself as being fat as a tick with deep southern roots where people still referred to sushi as bait. He was everyone's friend and everyone's enemy. People on The Hill confided in Graham only as a token to get more information from him. Graham's staff turnover rate was unbelievably high. In fact, he now had his first male secretary. It seemed no female was comfortable working for him. However, Graham managed to stay out of trouble and was never charged with any kind of misbehavior.

Graham was staring at a picture of his beach house when his secretary knocked.

"Majority Whip Scott Weston is here to see you, sir," the secretary informed him.

"Scott, old man," Graham said as he stood to shake Weston's hand aggressively. "How are the kids?"

"My kids are great. Nicole starts college this next fall, and Natalie is a sophomore in high school," Scott responded. While clearly uncomfortable in his chair, Senator Weston then took a deep breath and quickly continued, "Graham, it seems that there are some rumors floating around The Hill about you."

Graham's eyebrows instantly flared upward, and his eyes became as large as plates. "Scott, I am sure I don't know to what you are referring," Graham responded while sitting back down in his chair and crossing one leg over the other.

"Graham," Senator Weston stuttered, "it seems there are inquiries around some of the international trade and suppliers to the U.S. Some people are saying you are taking bribes or kickbacks to help Arkansas Governor Dobbs fund his campaign and to find favor with industry."

Senator Weston and Graham Barnes sat in the room in silence, staring at each other. Finally, Graham broke the infertile silence by getting up and offering his hand to Senator Weston. "Scott, you know me, and you know I'm a by-the-book kind of guy," Graham offered as he assisted Weston to a standing position. "I tell ya what: you go find those blabberers and bring them back to me; we will address them together."

Senator Weston, trembling, stood up and took a slap to the back by Graham. In a very agreeable manner he said, "Graham, I'm certain these things are rumors . . . just rumors. But I wanted you to know."

"No problem, Scott," Graham seethed as he ushered Senator Weston out the door. "Now, Scott, I will say this: if this is an attempt to sabotage me or Governor Dobbs, I am gonna jerk a knot in your tail."

They both stood only inches apart and stared at each other. Then Graham, in his Graham-spectacular way, laughed loudly and opened the door for Senator Weston.

"Scott let's get you on your way," he said jovially.

"Now, where is that boy?" Graham threw out into the air to no one in particular, referencing his new secretary. "I tell ya if that boy had an idea, it would die of loneliness."

At that, Graham ushered Majority Whip Weston into the hallway; and he returned to his desk.

*****

Governor Dobbs entered his office in a whirlwind. It was going to be yet another cold December and a very busy day on the campaign trail for the president. The governor powered up his laptop and then picked up his daily *Wall Street Journal*. He was old school in that manner: he preferred the paper version of the newspaper. He kicked back in his chair and indulged himself with a hot cup of coffee and his daily reading.

His cell phone rang. He picked it up out of annoyance and glanced at the caller ID. It was alarming to get a call from this particular person.

He tossed his beloved paper on the desk and answered sternly, "Hello."

"Tobias, I have to let you know it seems a body was discovered on Huck's property in October. No identification has been made yet. I can slow that process, but we need to be prepared for the worst," the caller said.

"Got it. Can you make it go away?" Governor Dobbs asked.

"Not this time . . . too many witnesses. And what makes it worse is now your friends from the Sahara are involved and may have been spotted," the caller continued.

Governor Dobbs rubbed his temple, feeling the start of a migraine.

"Have you contacted Graham?" Governor Dobbs inquired.

"No. You were the first call. I'll reach out to him, as well. Good luck on the election, Governor," the voice said before hanging up.

Governor Dobbs placed his cell phone on his desk. He spun his chair around to the window and gazed out of it for a moment. His office had to be one that was very mobile, as he travelled all the time, especially now gearing up for the campaign trail.

"People truly have no idea of the hardship of campaigning," he muttered under his breath.

But today was a lucky day as he sat at his home office. He could see the tall buildings of Little Rock in the far distance. He momentarily dismissed the memory of the call and rapidly returned his chair to the original station and retrieved his newspaper. He was back into his mind-numbing reading.

However, his subconscious mind still reeled from the phone conversation. As much as he tried to shake the conversation, he finally gave in and decided to give his campaign manager a call. He grabbed his phone from the desk a second time for the day.

"Good morning, Mr. President," the female voice on the other end very optimistically answered.

The governor chuckled and continued, "Good morning, Sofia. What good news do you have for me today?"

Sofia responded, "Sir, we have a new fundraiser we are scheduling with your secretary for next month. The holidays are always a great time for people to show their generosity."

"Good, good," the governor responded. "Sofia?"

"Yes, Governor," Sofia answered.

"Keep your eyes and ears open in case rumors bubble up," the governor more or less commanded.

"Certainly, Governor. Any particular rumors you think I should be aware of?" Sofia questioned.

"You know what I'm talking about," the governor replied and then hastily disconnected.

Sofia took a deep breath. Governor Tobias "Toby" Dobbs was her client. He had been a good client of hers for years. Only ten years ago he was just the Secretary of Agriculture for Arkansas, an appointed position that had proven quite lucrative in his search for political fame. Now, through trials and tribulations and clever work on her behalf, he was the governor . . . the governor who would likely be the next president of the United States with the election only two years out.

The Democrats from the south had all pulled together to rally their support for Toby. He was the perfect candidate: he was charming, quick-witted, wicked-smart in the economic realm, and slightly handsome. Of course, all politicians have their weaknesses, and his was living a lavish lifestyle.

"Rumors," she repeated to herself.

She stared across her neatly organized desk but didn't see anything. She breathed shallowly in and out for minutes. The solitude of her office was becoming her prison.

Sofia abruptly stood up and walked to her bookcase. Her bookcase housed not only books, but also pictures of some of the most influential people in American politics. She gazed on them one-by-one as she passed by.

Abruptly, she stopped and let her fingers carefully trace one specific picture frame. The picture that caught her attention was one of her team at a holiday celebration many years ago. She picked up the picture and slowly touched the image of a young man in the front row . . . a striking young man who was just an analyst for her then. Tall, dark hair, youthful grin . . . she truly missed him and felt a dull pain in her stomach as she thought about him.

Taking another deep breath, she set the frame back to its original perch. She then squared her shoulders and stepped back to her desk. Her mind raced, recalling the phone call she had just received. It had been easy to push those thoughts out of her mind all these years . . . the thoughts of what she had suspected had risen back to the forefront of her thoughts and would certainly become her nightmare tonight.

Of course, she thought back for what she was responsible. Her mind started working to justify her actions all those years ago.

However, even her thoughts betrayed her as they said, "Really? All you did was alert him that Dave was asking too many questions. If those questions were answered in the wrong media, would that destroy our presidential hopeful? It was the right thing to do as we must protect our candidate."

Chapter 23

As the sun rose, Jim inhaled a deep breath and filled his lungs with the sweet aroma of coffee that rolled from the door of his beloved coffee shop. After standing in euphoria for a few seconds, Jim quickly moseyed to the counter.

"Good morning, Mr. Jim," the young lady greeted. "The usual . . . or are you going to be adventurous today?"

Jim laughed and thought that maybe the barista's speaking to him this way was a sign of possible addiction.

"Yes, I'm living on the edge, so let's go crazy," Jim replied through his giant grin. "I think I will try the Red Eye."

The barista laughed, made change for him, and then proceeded to the side of the counter where nobody understood what happens; but in about three minutes, she would reappear with a cup of pure joy.

As Jim waited, he heard the voice he had grown to appreciate. "Professor Cunningham," Detective Garringer greeted the biologist.

Jim spun around to welcome Detective Garringer. "Good morning, Detective. May I buy you a drink?" Jim offered in a more than comical fashion.

Detective Garringer grinned out of sheer happiness that seemed to exist when she was around Jim.

"No thanks, Professor; I grabbed some java on my drive here this morning."

Jim motioned for the detective to have a seat while he clumsily gathered his drink from the young barista.

"Detective Garringer, I'm glad you could meet with me today. I'm certain you can understand my concerns about your case after Kat's and my experience last weekend," Jim started.

"Of course. That had to be very frightening for the both of you. I'm glad you called me after the two of you were attacked. How is Kat doing?" Detective Garringer inquired.

"I haven't spoken much to her since that day, but would like to. I mean I need to," Jim caught himself in a little transparent blip. "I'll call her after our meeting here today and update her. I'm sure she will feel better once I glean some information from you.

"So, what kind of updates might you have?" Jim pressed, all the time neglecting to look at Detective Garringer after his little mis-speak.

Detective Garringer remained in her quiet, professional demeanor. She slightly giggled at Jim's bumbling around the discussion of Kat. To be fair, Jim was talking to a detective; and determining his feelings for Kat needed very little investigative insight.

Detective Garringer finally answered, "Professor . . . I mean *Jim* . . . I have done some digging. This cold case just gets stranger the deeper I dig. The crime lab was unable to help me very much initially. I believe they had assumed Sheriff Drennan's theory of suicide was accurate and didn't pursue the investigation with any gusto."

"What does the crime lab say so far?" Jim asked.

"The preliminary report from the crime lab noted four significant injuries: the first was a comminuted fracture of the temporal lobe; the second, a 26mm hole on the top of the skull; and the third, the humerus was broken into three pieces. And of course, there was the C3 break in the neck. None of the injuries are suspected to be breakage by animal manipulation. Even knowing this, the preliminary report is showing 'inconclusive' cause of death," Detective Garringer explained disappointedly.

"So, the man takes a hit or hits to the side of his head, sustains some type of massive impact on the top of the head, and his arm was broken . . . how many times?" Jim thought out loud while rubbing the stubble on his face.

Detective Garringer nodded in agreement and took another sip of coffee.

"I have a theory, and I'll collect some DNA to test it; but I wanted to hear a little more about your encounter last weekend. Did you recognize the gentlemen who were shooting at you?"

"No, I had never seen them before. But one of our attackers carried a military-style weapon. I was a tad jealous, in fact," Jim replied.

"That's interesting," Detective Garringer said as she made notes in a notebook she kept on the ready. "What else did you notice?"

"Well, they were not speaking English . . . or even Spanish. I wouldn't know any other languages," Jim continued.

Detective Garringer continued to write in her notebook while Jim spoke.

Jim proceeded, "But I do have pictures of them from my drone."

Detective Garringer almost dropped her pen.

"You have pictures?" her voice quickened in speed as she repeated Jim's words.

Jim nodded as he answered, "They are not the greatest images because they are from my drone, but I downloaded them onto a thumbdrive that I brought with me."

He patted down his pockets in search of the illusive thumbdrive.

"Ah ha," Jim declared as he victoriously produced the thumbdrive and handed it over to Detective Garringer.

As she took the thumbdrive from Jim, she said, "I will have a friend from the FBI Drug Task Force take a look. If this is drug-related, he should know."

"Great," Jim responded. Then he very carefully and in a low, serious voice asked, "Detective Garringer, would you happen to have heard of a young man named Dave connected with Huck?"

Detective Garringer was stunned by Jim's question, and it showed on her very officially-trained, non-emotional face.

"Yes, I have heard of a young man named Dave Reid. Why do you ask?" she inquired.

"Detective Garringer, Kat told me a story. The story went something like this: Megan, Huck's daughter, fell in love with Dave. Dave and Huck didn't like each other . . . even had a falling out of some kind. Kat felt Dave was going to ask Megan to marry him. She thought maybe Dave made a special trip to Huck's house to mend things . . . but I don't think Dave did that."

"Why?" Detective Garringer simply asked.

"Because the morning that Kat and I were attacked, I found this," Jim said as he pulled the tiny, rusted pill box from his pants pocket.

He opened it to show the fragile, yet exquisite, solitaire ring. Detective Garringer's eyes lit up—more out of confusion than anything.

Jim continued, "When I showed Kat this box, she said she had seen it before. Dave brought it by to show her—just the box, not the ring. He told Kat he had a present for Megan. Megan never got the box; I found it on the bluff . . . the bluff that is directly above the cave where the body was found. Detective Garringer, that boy has apparently been missing for some time. I truly don't think it was a result of Huck's buying him off. The rumor Kat heard was Huck was trying to send him to the Sahara, but I don't think he ever left the U.S."

Detective Garringer sat back in her chair as though someone had knocked the wind out of her chest.

"Jim, you are correct. I have a lead that Dave Reid was missing. I tracked down his family. Unfortunately, I did find a flight manifest that shows Dave flew from Boston to Morocco in October 2010. But I'm suspicious that whoever flew that day was not Dave Reid. May I have the box so I can test DNA at the crime lab?"

"Of course," Jim replied as he handed her the box.

"Jim, who knows you were attacked?" Detective Garringer asked through piercing eyes.

Jim, somewhat stunned by the question, simply replied, "Nobody . . . well, besides you and Sheriff Drennan."

"Who knows you discovered this box?" she continued.

Again, Jim's simple answer was, "Nobody . . . not even Drennan."

Detective Garringer, in a low, firm voice said, "Good! Jim, this is getting serious . . . possibly dangerous. You cannot tell anyone—even Sheriff Drennan—about our discoveries."

Jim nodded his head, affirming Detective Garringer's wishes. Detective Garringer stood up.

"Professor Cunningham," she said as she gathered her things, "the body is that of Dave Reid. I know that just like you do. I just don't know how or why. But I assure you, I *will* find out."

_Chapter 24

Detective Garringer left Jim's treasured coffee shop and stepped into her car. Her thoughts kept running through her head, "Dave Reid is missing. Is it possible someone faked his trip to Morocco to cover up a kidnapping or possible murder? What did Huck Ferguson have to do with this? What was the falling out about that they had?"

This cold case was certainly taking up a lot of her time, but she knew she needed more information . . . and the first item on her checklist was to get these images to her friend to see if he knew anything about these people.

She called her longtime friend, Brian Pinick, who was the director at the 4th District Drug Task Force in Fayetteville. "Hi, Brian. This is Lori. Look, I really need your help identifying a perpetrator who may be linked to drugs, here and abroad."

That certainly got his attention; however, when she went on to give Brian more of the information she had already gathered, he was adamant in his suggestion, "Lori, I'm clearing my calendar for the rest of the afternoon. If you can get in here as quickly as you can, I will give you whatever time you need."

It had been a tough call for Detective Garringer to make. She knew she needed someone she could trust, and she believed Brian fit the bill. They had met at college, the University of Arkansas. In fact, they were actually a couple back in those days. She remembered how determined Brian was. He had totally indulged himself in the poli-sci movement. He clearly loved everything he could learn. The only breaks he would take would be those to come watch her run in her track meets. He was such a powerful support mechanism for her.

"What ever happened to us?" she thought as she drove toward his Fayetteville office.

Almost an hour later, Detective Garringer walked into the Criminal Investigation Office close to the artsy Fayetteville Square. Detective Garringer always giggled to herself as she found it ironic that such a beautiful, scenic part of downtown Fayetteville also housed one of the busiest drug task forces in Arkansas.

Brian was walking down the hall, coffee in hand, when he caught sight of Detective Garringer.

"Come on in, Lori," Brian motioned to her.

Brian was a thin, very fit, tanned, attractive man with salt-and-pepper hair. The years had been kind to him. He had ice-blue eyes hidden behind black-rimmed glasses, which did nothing but set off the blue even more. His five o'clock shadow only enhanced his mysterious appearance. She had heard he was a real charmer with the ladies, and she could see why. Her heart gave a little flutter.

Detective Garringer followed Brian into one of the most understated offices—even compared to hers—that she had ever seen. There was not one picture on any wall, desk, end table—had there been one—or even on a bookcase. Brian's desk had very few documents on it. His computer was powered up, and his keyboard showed signs of wear and tear . . . maybe even a victim of a coffee spill or two. He had one large filing cabinet in the corner with a small stack of files on top . . . no diploma, no certificates, no commendations of which she knew he had earned many—almost nothing anywhere.

There were two simple and very tattered guest chairs available. Lori grabbed one and started digging for the thumbdrive even as she lowered herself into the chair. She had trouble locating the thumbdrive and felt a bit dazed as she had never struggled finding anything before.

"Jim's absent-minded professor mentality must be contagious," she thought to herself and chuckled.

Of course, she finally found the thumbdrive stuffed deep into the side pocket of her backpack.

"Lori, it's been years! You look great, by the way. What

brings you up to Northwest Arkansas?" Brian said as he sat his coffee on his desk and settled into his chair.

"Yes, it has certainly been a long time. Your suit looks nice; I didn't picture you as a suit guy," Detective Garringer responded, almost gushing.

"Well, I'm not a suit guy. Ha! My sister took over my wardrobe selection a few years ago. She said if I wanted to start getting noticed, I needed to look the part. Thanks for noticing," Brian sheepishly explained.

"I heard you recently made a small drug bust at the University. Congratulations! Working on anything exciting?"

"Lori, I am always working on something exciting," Brian chuckled as he sat further back into his chair and peered over the rim of his glasses.

They both stared at each other until the silence became awkward.

"Listen, I was deployed to a crime scene in October in Cherokee City. I feel there is a larger connection than maybe what our crime lab is currently reporting. I could really use your help. Could you pull this image up and tell me if you recognize anyone?" she very tactfully explained.

Brian retrieved the thumbdrive from Detective Garringer and pulled up the video images. He watched very carefully as he was a man of detail. When the images of the two men came into view, Brian stopped the video and enlarged it as much as he could with the equipment at his desk. He paused and held his chin in his hand, his eyes glued to the screen. Detective Garringer waited quietly as she didn't want to disrupt Brian's process, as something had clearly caught his attention.

"Yes Lori, I may know who at least one of them is," Brian finally responded after several minutes, which seemed like an hour to Detective Garringer.

Excitement rumbled through her body. She was hoping Brian could give her a lead, but she didn't expect him to say he knew the people in the image.

"Where did you say this video came from?" Brian questioned.

Detective Garringer moved to the edge of her chair while watching Brian with intensity.

She continued, "As I said, I was deployed to a crime scene in Cherokee City in early October. The local sheriff dismissed the John Doe as a victim of a drug crime or possibly suicide. I suspect there is more to the story. A local hiker has since provided evidence that made me question if the assailants were pursuing some kind of evidence from a prior offense. In fact, the hiker was attacked by these men. I was given this video and have been asked for help. I'm certain you can understand that, at the moment, I have to protect the informant until I better understand what we are dealing with."

Brian moved his gaze from the computer screen to Detective Garringer as she revealed her concerns.

"So, the hiker has found something?" Brian interrupted.

"No, I don't think so," Detective Garringer responded, thinking his question was a bit odd. "I believe those two men *think* he has found something."

She felt the need to blur the truth to protect Jim and Kat. Again, that sixth sense that had always proven itself strong appeared in her head. Brian's gaze returned to the screen, chin still in hand.

"I don't really understand why this man—if he is who I think he is—would be in this area of the state. Honestly, I'll need to dig into some surveillance to verify; but he looks to be a gentleman we have had on a watch list for phosphate trades and drug trafficking from the Sahara."

Detective Garringer's mind spun.

"Phosphate? Like . . . he is creating bombs?" she questioned.

Brian's gaze never left the screen, but he nodded to confirm.

"We have several commodity traders we monitor in alliance with Homeland Security. Phosphate is one of those commodities. What makes it difficult is determining how much of the commodity is traded for agricultural use and how much is stockpiled to sell to terrorist cells," Brian further explained.

Detective Garringer started piecing together her own little narrative.

"Commodities . . . commodities for agricultural use. Are you telling me, you are monitoring fertilizer traders?" Detective Garringer sarcastically quizzed.

Brian then looked over to Lori and saw her narrowed eyes. He knew she knew something more.

"Yes—in a roundabout way—we are monitoring phosphate trades used in fertilizer and phosphate that could also be used to blow up the Superbowl!" Brian responded equally sarcastically. "Why? Do you know something else?" he pushed.

Detective Garringer made a couple of notes in her notebook, avoiding Brian's gaze. Her thoughts took her back to the statement that Jim had made, "Dave and Huck had had it out over something. Could Huck, a successful commodity trader, be feeding phosphate to terror cells?"

Realizing Brian was still staring at her, waiting for her to answer his question, she cleared her throat and responded, "Oh, I don't know that I know anything else. The only thing I do know is you have just made this case more complicated. Who is the man you recognize?"

Brian returned his gaze to the video and answered, "We call him Ben. I would have to look up his official name. Something like Bin Moussir."

"Where is Ben from?" Detective Garringer asked.

"He is from the Sahara . . . I am thinking Morocco, the land of mines . . . phosphate mines," Brian answered. "To be honest, Lori, that's all I know. But I'm happy to dig into this some more for you. Is it okay if I keep this video? I am assuming more copies exist?" Brian tactfully and diplomatically responded, hoping to elicit more information from her.

"Of course. Keep it. When you have more information, I would appreciate it if you would contact me," Detective Garringer stated matter-of-factly and avoided answering the "copies" question.

She started to gather her notebook into her backpack and stood to leave.

"No hurry to rush off, Lori. It's close to five o'clock now; let's go grab a drink," Brian charmingly invited. "We can catch up on old times."

"Ha! No, Brian. I would love to, but I need to start my drive back to the Rock. Another time?"

"Of course, and I'll hold you to that," Brian responded as he lit up a brilliant smile.

Detective Garringer exited Brian's office in a quick but confident pace. She needed to talk to Jim.

_____ Chapter 25

On Detective Garringer's drive home, she made a mental note that she needed to delve further into the topic of fertilizer. She decided she would put off calling Jim until she had a little more information on it, certain she would be asking him some nature-type questions.

Upon arriving at her apartment close to three hours later, she tossed her keys onto the side table, glancing slightly at the shadowbox as she walked past. She pulled out her laptop from her backpack and settled on the couch after kicking off her shoes.

"Where to begin?" she thought.

She immediately Googled "Huck Ferguson" only to discover two very unique links: one was to Ferguson Brokers, a commodity firm in Little Rock; the other was SP Industries, LLC. That one caught her attention as she was expecting only a commodity brokerage; so, this was new information. She had read a reference regarding SP Industries earlier in the investigation but had failed to research it further.

Huck Ferguson was listed as a member of the Board of Directors for SP Industries. SP Industries was at one point a fairly large company, consisting of over 200 people. The company was founded in 1998. They were a distributor of fertilizer throughout the south but primarily focused on the delta. It had been decreasing in employees and assets since 2012 and, ultimately, sold in 2015, the same year the cabin property had been purchased.

"The selling of fertilizer seems to be a fairly lucrative business. Who knew?" the detective half said out loud.

It seemed SP Industries was a bit static in sales from 1998-2005. For whatever reason, SP Industries grew drastically from 2006-2011. The big year was 2007. It more than doubled in size and sales.

"I wonder what made SP Industries the fertilizer company of choice," Detective Garringer muttered to herself. "Actually, what *makes* good fertilizer?" she said as she rolled her eyes. "I'm a detective and in the muck . . . literally," she said out loud as if someone could hear her. "Again, follow the money."

Huck was known for his lavish parties to raise campaign funds for Governor Dobbs. So, money had to come from somewhere. Could the money have come from fertilizer sales?

Switching gears, she went back to the original search result for Huck Ferguson. Huck was still listed on the Directory of Commodity Brokers; however, the contact info led to the commodity firm, Ferguson Brokers, rather than to Huck directly. The firm seemed to have been decreasing in assets starting in 2012, the same as SP Industries. It seemed as though the list of brokers who worked for the firm had dwindled to almost zero by 2018.

She decided to dig into political donations from SP Industries, LLC, and Ferguson Brokers, still looking for the connection to Governor Dobbs. Accessing this information proved challenging. Corporate returns were confidential. She would have to have a subpoena to view the records . . . and to make matters worse, being a corporation, they could donate to a PAC; and those dollars were near impossible to trace.

"Where is Huck?" Detective Garringer asked out loud. "Where, oh, where are you?"

She researched property records, looking for a residence. A $1.2 million-dollar sale was recorded in 2016. The sale referenced a 4,500-square-foot home on five acres near Maumelle, Arkansas. No other residences in Arkansas were listed post 2016.

"So, where are you?" Detective Garringer again mumbled out loud. "Assuming that was your primary home—and for goodness sake, why wouldn't it be—and you sold the cabin to the Moores, where did you go from there?" Detective Garringer pondered.

"Maybe it is time to give Megan, Huck's daughter, a call," Detective Garringer thought, mentally switching gears. "However, if there is anything to cover up, typically close family members cover. But at least she could answer as to where Huck is."

Detective Garringer started a search for "Jacquelin Vanderli," aka Megan Ferguson. She found Jacquelin's work website and quickly put in a call to the agent. Unfortunately, she had to leave a message.

Trying to sound very professional and not a bit alarming in the message, Detective Garringer said, "This is Detective Garringer from the Arkansas State Police. I am following up on a cold case and may have found some property belonging to Megan . . . or Jacquelin as she now is known. Could you ask her to call me tomorrow?"

Detective Garringer was fairly certain that call would not be returned. She pondered yet again on how to gain information regarding Huck Ferguson from 2015 to present. She continued to sit on her couch as she looked at the Bill of Sale for his home in Maumelle.

"An estate that large has to have caretakers," she thought. "I will take a quick drive there tomorrow and see if I can uncover any past caretakers."

Detective Garringer closed her laptop and slowly performed her nightly ritual only to crawl into bed already half asleep before her head hit the pillow.

Lori's mind again slipped into dreams of her very early childhood. Lori had strong, precious, warm memories of her father, especially at night, which may be why she dreamed so often of him. Her father had always been so sweet; he always tucked Lori and her brother into bed. She dreamed about how she would say to him, "Tell me the story of our Indian princess, Bird." Her father would peer down into his daughter's deep, dark, and very determined eyes. Those eyes held his heart as they were certainly the same eyes of his beloved wife. He would smile, which was a rarity, and start the story.

"Banaysheug," he said, using the Iroquois word for "little bird" and his nickname for her, "why must you hear this story every night?"

She would always answer, "Because I want to be a warrior princess, just like your people."

He would take a deep breath, lay his long body down next to her with his feet hanging over the side of her bed, and start his story while staring at the ceiling as though he was telling the story to the gods.

"A long, very long time ago before America was America, the soldiers came to the land of our tribe. One of the white soldiers who fought the British was Claude Phillip Ezell. He was a noble soldier. He was respectful to our ancestors' ways. He made friends with the younger warriors of the tribe by often alerting the tribe of possible attacks. Eventually, the warriors rewarded Claude and invited him to their banquet with the elders. That is where he met Chief Grey Wolf. Chief Grey Wolf was a fierce leader who cherished and protected his people. He had many sons but only one daughter, Banaysheug. She stood by his side during the banquet. Claude saw her and immediately fell in love with her. She stood as tall as her brothers. She was intelligent and fearless as she challenged her brothers when they chanted in favor of war."

Lori's father would turn his head to look at his daughter often as he told his story, maybe to see if she was sleeping . . . maybe just to gaze at her uniqueness, sweetness, and childlike delicacy.

He continued with his story, "Claude found many reasons to visit the tribe . . . but always he wanted to see Banaysheug. He saw her one day running through the forest. He thought she was being chased. So, he ran after her to protect her. He lost sight of her at a clearing which surrounded a great lake. He then heard her laughing. He tried to find her, but only after she decided to let him see her did he finally see her. She asked him why he was chasing her. He told her between gasps for air that he was protecting her."

Propping himself up on one elbow, he looked into his daughter's face as he said, "She was much like you, Banaysheug. She could outrun any of her brothers. That's why we call you Banaysheug." Every time Lori's father mentioned her namesake, she smiled with pride.

He continued his story yet again, "Claude married Banaysheug. They had many children, all who were hard workers and warriors. You come from a long line of proud people, Banaysheug. Grow up to make them proud."

When he got to that point, Lori was typically asleep. His challenge was then to get his long body off her bed without waking her up.

_____Chapter 26

Detective Garringer awoke with energy. Her full night's rest had revigorated her. Her mind was clear; she was focused.

She climbed into her car, set the GPS for Huck's old homestead in Maumelle, and headed out on her journey. Only once did she sidetrack so she could grab a soda from Sonic to get her caffeine boost.

She finally arrived at the estate. The one picture she had found of the house did not do it justice. The Tuscan-style home boasted two stories, possibly with a walk-out basement. One was met with warmly colored walls with natural color influences. The walls were grand, tall, and finished in stucco. Arches designated the entrances and flowed over terra cotta walkways. It reeked of elegance.

She rang the doorbell which was positioned next to two large, front doors with iron accents. She could hear footsteps hurriedly approaching the door. A somewhat seasoned-in-age lady with a giant smile answered the door.

"Can I help you?" she asked with a wonderful, southern accent.

"Yes," Detective Garringer responded while presenting her badge. "I am investigating a cold case and believe I have found some property that belongs to a Huck Ferguson, the former owner of this house. I was wondering if you could help me with some questions as to his whereabouts," Detective Garringer spouted, just as she had rehearsed on her drive.

"I'm sorry, I cannot help you; I do not know a Mr. Ferguson," the lady answered. "Unfortunately, the current owner of the house is not available, either," she added.

Detective Garringer nodded, as she almost expected that response.

"By chance, do you know any of the previous caretakers?" she asked.

The lady nodded and became excited as she appeared to be glad to help law enforcement the best she could.

"As a matter of fact, I do know the groundskeeper. He worked for the owners here for a long time; his name is Chris Stone. He has since taken on more jobs in this growing community. I believe he also works for the neighbor two houses down on the right," she said as she motioned in that direction.

Detective Garringer thanked her and got back into her car. She drove down two houses, which was quite a distance when each estate was five-plus acres. She pulled into a beautiful, more southern-style estate. The house had a wraparound porch with rocking chairs everywhere. The driveway was immaculate. The remnants of what once was a carefully manicured lawn lay dormant.

She parked and exited her car. She noticed a truck and trailer nested by the large metal barn off to the side of the estate. The truck was wrapped with "Stone Landscaping - We Rock You."

Detective Garringer followed the sound of a lawn mower from around the back side of the house. She quickly saw what appealed to this landowner: an amazing view of the lake while the house was situated in the shelter of trees to retain its privacy. The lake was moving just slightly under the December wind. No boats were in sight, which made the view even more breathtaking. She could see the cove on the other side, imagining how scenic this would be once the trees regained their leaves in the spring.

She was shaken back into reality when she heard the lawnmower approach. She smiled and waved the man to a stop.

"Can I help you?" he asked very politely.

"Yes. I am Detective Garringer with the Arkansas State Police."

Again, she presented her badge.

"I am working on a cold case where I may have discovered some property belonging to Huck Ferguson. I would like to get that to him, but I am unable to ascertain his whereabouts," she said, using the same line as before, making good use of her rehearsal in the car. "I was told you used to work for Mr. Ferguson," she suggested.

"Yes, as a matter of fact, I worked for him for something like eight years. He was a great guy, gave me lots of referrals, and helped me build my business," he stated proudly. "They sold his house . . . maybe three years or so ago," he continued.

"Yes . . . do you know where he is now?" Detective Garringer inquired.

"Last I heard, his daughter, Megan, took him to Los Angeles to live with her. He is lucky to have family to take care of him in his condition," he explained.

That statement caught Detective Garringer's attention.

"Condition?" she prompted.

"You know . . . dementia. I tell ya, Huck was a great man. Such a shame that this happened to him," he continued while checking his mower deck.

Detective Garringer was almost dumbfounded.

"Dementia . . . a fate worse than death," swirled through her mind. "Was he diagnosed?" she asked.

"I guess so; I know for about two years he was making mistakes and forgetting things. Things got kinda heated when he was charged by the SEC. That's when Megan showed up," he said, shaking his head with pity.

"Do you know what he was charged with? Detective Garringer asked.

"No . . . never asked," Mr. Stone responded.

Detective Garringer nodded in understanding and thanked Mr. Stone for the information.

Just as she was preparing to leave, she turned and asked, "Why are you mowing in December?"

He chuckled and answered, "I'm not mowing; I'm mulching all the dead leaves. This house is great, and the owners can't stand to see any dead leaves on their lawn. I'm happy to oblige," Mr. Stone said with a grin and a wink.

Detective Garringer got back into her car and returned to her office by late afternoon with only one more stop to Sonic for another dose of caffeine. She was kicking herself: she had never thought to run any kind of court record check on Huck Ferguson until the caretaker had stated that Huck Ferguson had been charged by the SEC.

"Rookie mistake," she scolded herself.

She pulled up the court records to discover that yes, Mr. Stone was, in fact, correct: on June 2, 2014, a civil suit was filed in Pulaski County alleging misrepresentation or omission of important securities information against Lawrence Huck Ferguson. As she followed the case, she became intrigued. The case was quickly dropped in August 2014. She assumed it was settled before going to court.

Detective Garringer sat back in her chair and began reviewing in her mind all the details she knew of this case: a body had been found on Huck Ferguson's land in 2018; Sheriff Drennan believed it to be a suicide, which could not be correct; Dave Reid, former boyfriend of Megan Ferguson, Huck Ferguson's daughter, had been missing since 2010; Huck's daughter sold the land where the body was found in 2015; Huck had had some kind of dementia since at least 2014; Huck, in the past, raised significant dollars to help Governor Dobbs' campaign; and Governor Dobbs is currently running for president of the United States.

"Who is protecting whom?" she questioned out loud.

_____Chapter 27

The next morning Lori returned to her apartment after a quick run. Her cell phone rang. Caller ID displayed a strange area code, 213.

She answered, "Lori Garringer." Though a bit breathless, she managed a professional sound to her greeting.

"Detective Garringer?" a very timid and soft-spoken female responded on the other end. "This is Megan Ferguson. I believe you phoned my manager about some property."

Detective Garringer was caught off guard. She struggled to focus as this call was unexpected. She found herself stammering. She again became very disappointed in herself.

Finally, finding her bearings, she responded, "Megan! Thank you for returning my call. Yes, I am investigating a cold case. I'm actually uncertain the exact year of the homicide."

With that last statement, she heard a small gasp on the other end of the phone. She paused slightly so Megan could regain her composure.

"Yes, my team made a discovery on land owned by your dad. We are currently following leads," the detective resumed.

"Detective Garringer, I sold that land to Charles Moore over three years ago. I'm certain your cold case is more suited to be focused on him."

"Yes," Detective Garringer continued with the utmost diplomacy. "We are following all leads. Can you tell me when you were there last?"

"Of course. It was when I met the real estate agent in 2015 to sign documents and complete the move of my dad's belongings," Megan stated. "You see, Detective, my dad was diagnosed with Alzheimer's in 2013. Sadly, I didn't know until more than a year later. After I discovered his illness, I brought him to live with me here in Los Angeles."

"I am very sorry, Ms. Ferguson," Detective Garringer stated as she was eagerly pulling notepads off her coffee table to take notes.

"Don't be, Detective. I've come to grips with Dad's illness . . . and it is an illness. His mind has quit functioning. There are some good days left, but few. I cherish those moments when he recognizes me. I even cherish the moments he calls me Kerry, who was my mother."

Detective Garringer was taken aback by Megan's acceptance of her dad's illness. Although Megan sounded weak—or even meek—on the phone, clearly, she was a woman of strength to have found solace in the midst of this devastating disease.

Realizing the awkward silence, Detective Garringer continued as she rummaged through things, searching for a pen, "Ms. Ferguson, are you currently in Los Angeles?"

"Yes, I am," Megan answered.

"Would it be something like 5 a.m. there right now?" Detective Garringer pushed, heaving a bit of a sigh of relief having now located all materials for notetaking.

"Yes, I am finishing up a shoot. You see, my films are better to be shot at night. It sets a better feel for suspense," Megan very meekly responded.

"I see. When was the last time you know your dad was present at the cabin?"

"I am not completely certain. I packed him up from his Maumelle home in 2014. My guess would be that year. Detective Garringer, you mentioned to my agent you had possibly found some property that was mine. What was that?"

Detective Garringer took a deep breath.

"We found a small, antique pill box with some jewelry in it."

"I don't recall missing a box or jewelry. Where did you find it?" Megan questioned.

"We actually found it on a trail toward the bluff overlooking Huck's cabin."

Complete silence. Detective Garringer checked her phone to verify she still had a connection.

After what seemed minutes, but was likely seconds, Detective Garringer broke the silence, "Ms. Ferguson? Are you still there?"

"Yes," Megan responded quickly.

"Would you like to see the box to verify ownership?" Detective Garringer asked.

"No . . . wait . . . yes, I would like to see it. In fact, I will be back to Cherokee City in two weeks for the holidays with Kat. Can we visit then?" Megan asked, but this time her voice cracked.

"I would be happy to meet you somewhere," Detective Garringer responded.

Finally, Megan asked very bluntly, "Did you find someone's body?"

"Yes," Detective Garringer stated, "but that body has not been positively identified. Do you have any idea who it could be?"

"I don't know. I'm not entirely sure I want to know," Megan quickly added.

She was clearly walking now as Detective Garringer could hear her shuffling something around. Then Detective Garringer sensed the unmistakable sound of quiet tears.

"Ms. Ferguson, if you have any idea who our John Doe could be, please let me know," Detective Garringer requested.

"Yes . . . yes, of course," Megan stammered. "I am just a little surprised. I was expecting you to ask about something totally different," Megan added in an almost trance-like state.

Those words were not what Detective Garringer expected, either. Her senses heightened as she couldn't believe what she was hearing.

"What do you mean?" Detective Garringer insisted.

"Oh . . . it's probably nothing. My dad keeps saying the Old Dominion is in power. I have no idea what that even means. I honestly don't even know if he knows what he is saying. But he has been saying it since October," Megan rattled off.

Megan abruptly changed to an attitude of gusto. "Detective

Garringer, thank you for your time. I will text you a time and place we can meet when I arrive. Is that okay?"

"Of course, Ms. Ferguson," Detective Garringer responded. "Please be safe in your travels, and please feel free to call me any time, day or night, if you have questions or concerns," Detective Garringer offered. Realizing how diplomatic and impersonal that sounded, she quickly followed with, "Megan, I mean that. Please be safe, and please keep my number close," she reemphasized.

"Yes," Megan simply replied and hung up.

_____Chapter 28

Feeling she had hit a brick wall, Detective Garringer decided to switch her target entirely.

"Maybe Toby is connected to Huck instead of Huck connected to Toby," she muttered out loud.

Detective Garringer sat on her couch, tapping her finger on the keyboard, thinking in rhythm. She felt she had to start somewhere, so she just simply Googled "Tobias Dobbs." She found numerous links to current policy, campaigning speeches, and rallies; but she was much more interested in his distant past. She pulled up an old interview from the time he was running for governor as the cabinet-appointed Secretary of Agriculture. She scrolled through the interview questions. The questions were simple ones, such as "What are your plans for Arkansas, if elected?"

His response: "To grow the Arkansas state gross domestic product. Our state is thriving with business and industry, not to mention our substantial investment and opportunities in agriculture. It's time our state offers tax breaks to these enterprises and expands its reach," Tobias replied.

That statement seemed to catch Detective Garringer's attention. She always felt Governor Dobbs had a strong economic head on him and truly made a difference for the state. She continued to read the article.

"What background do you have that will prepare you for the governor role?" the reporter had asked.

"Obviously, serving eight years as Secretary of Agriculture has provided me with the opportunity to learn this role, meet the people who engage in the political environment, and get comfortable with policy process. But more importantly, I look back to my years as an analyst for Carver and Company. I was blessed with great mentors from my early days in business. Mr. Carver was always a supporter . . . one who taught me to take risks . . . a man whom I miss terribly since his premature death in 2003," Governor Dobbs had replied.

"Carver?" Detective Garringer repeated in her mind. "That's right! Mr. Quinn stated he introduced Toby to Huck back in the days when Quinn worked for Carver. Toby must have worked for Carver, as well."

"Risks?" Detective Garringer thought to herself, picking up on another word in Dobbs' answer to the reporter. "I wonder if Toby truly did take risks?"

Out of a complete hunch, she pulled up the county clerk info that she could access. She had only limited access . . . like the civilian ranks. She searched for any land purchases by Tobias Dobbs in 1988-1998.

"Bingo!" she cried out.

There were large tracts of land that Tobias Dobbs had purchased in Maumelle, Arkansas. It appeared he paid full market price in 1997. As she tracked the land, she discovered the land sold to SP Industries, LLC, in 1999. That appeared interesting.

"Why would someone buy land at full market price in 1997 only to sell in 1999?" Detective Garringer asked herself. "And why Maumelle?"

She looked at her watch. It displayed 11:34 p.m. It was late. But she was wired after the day she had. She picked up her phone and made the call.

"So, now you are calling me in the middle of the night?" Jim's raspy voice responded.

Detective Garringer couldn't help but giggle.

"Yes, your charm keeps me awake. Listen, I have some news. I promised that I would update you, but the time slipped away from me."

"Oka-a-a-y," Jim responded very slowly.

Detective Garringer continued, "It seems the guys who were hunting you were from Morocco and have some strange connection to the phosphate mines."

"Um, what?" Jim was puzzled. "You mean, like fertilizer for crops or boom-boom phosphate?"

Detective Garringer couldn't help but laugh again.

"I am uncertain at the moment. Let me continue. I've done some more research. It seems Huck Ferguson is connected . . . at least on the fertilizer side. But I know Huck was a big campaign guy for Governor Dobbs back in the day when he was running for governor . . . not to mention they have had some land deals together. I smell a stink."

"Detective Garringer, remember I told you Kat's story of Dave going to Morocco and never being seen again?" Jim uttered, now wide awake and sitting on the edge of his bed.

"Yes, I remember. There is definitely something that ties Dave to Morocco, Morocco to Huck, and now I am wondering about Governor Dobbs, not to mention Dave's previous boss, Sofia," Detective Garringer recounted. "Jim, to be safe, be on guard. In all my years of investigations, this one is more complicated and eviler than all the others. I'm thinking this is not a crime of passion, self-defense, or even anger. This appears to be more calculated. I just need to figure out who is punching the keys."

Jim agreed to be careful and disconnected with Detective Garringer. He pulled the covers back up around his neck . . . now wide awake. He turned to see Jax sitting in his corner bed, head lowered, staring up at him.

"What's wrong with you? Did I disrupt your beauty sleep?" Jim joked.

After lying in bed a few minutes, he reached over and pulled a gun out of the drawer. He ejected the magazine to verify the presence of bullets, replaced the magazine, and returned the gun to its haven. He rubbed his forehead.

"This is getting serious, now," he thought to himself. "I should've gone to work as a game warden," he mumbled and rolled over to try to regain some sleep.

Chapter 29

Detective Garringer returned to work with her head full of scenarios. Huck Ferguson was a great and mighty commodity broker; he seemed very successful. He and Sofia Agassi were a bit of a power couple in regard to getting the right people from the South elected. One of their candidates was Governor Dobbs. But how was Governor Dobbs and Huck Ferguson really connected?

Detective Garringer was so caught up in her thoughts she didn't realize her captain had entered the room.

"Detective Garringer?" Captain Lambert announced in a commanding voice.

Detective Garringer, startled by his sudden appearance, jumped, knocking over her coffee cup.

"You seem extra jumpy, Detective," Captain Lambert responded with an accusatory tone.

"Sorry, you startled me," Detective Garringer defended herself.

"Listen, Lori, I'm here as a concerned friend. It seems you have been letting some things slip through the cracks here at work. And then I get a message from some Mrs. Reid in St. Louis . . . which is in *Missouri* in case you have lost your globe," Captain Lambert added harshly. "I also find out that you are digging into donations to the Democratic party and researching fertilizer companies. I *have* to start asking, 'Why?'"

Detective Garringer started to speak.

"Don't!" Captain Lambert stopped her and held up his hand. "As your boss, I'm telling you to just stop. Get yourself refocused on your current case load. We have people to handle this cold case."

Detective Garringer nodded in affirmation, mainly just hoping Captain Lambert would leave her office so she could get back to her research. The captain gave Detective Garringer that "caught you" look as he strutted out of her office.

Detective Garringer took a couple of breaths to regain her focus. She glanced back at her computer as she replayed in her mind the captain's commands: "I also find out that you are digging into donations to the Democratic party and researching fertilizer companies."

Detective Garringer stopped for a moment, reliving that sentence from Captain Lambert: "researching fertilizer companies." How did Captain Lambert know she had Googled fertilizer companies? Why did Captain Lambert choose today to confront her?

Detective Garringer had an eerie feeling that this was not happenstance. She now knew her computer had been compromised. She picked up her phone to reach out to Jim and warn him, as one government employee to another, to be careful what he sent via his computer. But she stopped a moment and looked at her phone. The realization hit her. Her captain reported *directly* to the governor. She should be more careful about what her boss knew. Also, the more times she reached out to Jim via phone would put Jim in danger. If her computer had truly been compromised, her phone certainly had been, as well. She must find a way to communicate with Jim in a non-alerting fashion . . . just in case.

As Detective Garringer sat pondering, an email popped up regarding her case eReports. The crime lab had completed its DNA check on the ring. They had submitted the DNA to the database and would alert her of a match as soon as possible.

Detective Garringer sat at her desk, raking her fingers across her keyboard. There was a lot she could not do in this world, but one thing she *could* do was bring closure where possible. She picked up her cell phone to make a dreaded call to St. Louis to update a grieving brother.

With that, Detective Garringer made a quick drive to the crime lab to retrieve the ring by signing it out of evidence.

As Detective Garringer drove home later that night, she was more on alert than before. If someone from the bureau was tracking her, they would do it via her phone and GPS. No longer were the days of trailing someone with a car.

"Surely, I am overreacting," thought Detective Garringer to herself.

She opened the door to her apartment and dropped her keys into the bowl. She set down her backpack, as was her routine. She spontaneously decided to go for a run to remove the excess jitters. She changed clothes, slipped her gun into her shoulder holster under her coat, and started to grab her phone. She stood, holding her phone, questioning her earlier fears from the morning. After a long moment of waffling, she placed the phone back on the counter, grabbed her keys, and left.

"If you are going to trail me, you're gonna have to do it the old-fashioned way," she whispered to herself as she started her jog through downtown Little Rock.

When she returned from her run, she picked up her phone to check for messages. She had received one text that she had been expecting . . . and somewhat dreading. The message simply read, "I will be at Kat's house Friday through the weekend. Can we meet? Megan."

It would be Detective Garringer's chance to deliver the ring, as well as ask some incredibly emotional and tough questions.

_____Chapter 30

Brian arrived at his office early on Saturday morning. Even though he was early to the office, he still managed to dress in a very coordinated Under Armor sweatshirt and jogging pants. Every hair was in place, and he was clean shaven.

He settled into his desk chair and powered up his computer. While waiting for the computer to resume full power, he sipped on his Starbucks drink. Once his machine was accessible, Brian started thumbing through the video he had received during Detective Garringer's visit. He played the video in slow motion, watching one of the two male hunters.

Brian wasn't focused only on facial recognition of the tall man; he was watching what the man was doing. The man was clearly looking through the brush for something. His companion was using a metal detector. The fact that they were there and armed meant they were looking for something specific . . . and that something had to be important enough to bring the shorter guy here. Brian continued sitting in his chair, rubbing his chin, deep in thought.

"Hey, Brian," a voice seemed to almost scream into his office.

Brian jumped out of shock. One of his junior agents happened to be walking through.

"Hello, Kellie Jo," Brian said.

Kellie Jo seemed to illuminate. It was obvious that she had a crush on Brian since her first week on the job.

"What are you doing here on a Saturday?" Brian asked, trying to cover the fact she caught him in a defenseless moment.

"Oh, I had some paperwork to follow up on regarding that drug bust on the campus last month," Kellie Jo replied.

She shuffled through the stack of papers in her arms while glancing back and forth from Brian to the papers.

"I see," Brian continued in more of a mentoring voice. "Well, I don't want to keep you. I can only imagine you have big plans for this evening."

Kellie Jo found herself caught off guard momentarily, then very flirtatiously said, "Well, no . . . um . . . not really. I don't think so."

Catching the cues, Brian decided he needed to head off the potential crush and get back to something much more important.

"Well, Kellie Jo, I don't want to distract you any further. I'll be leaving here in just a moment; hopefully, you can get out of here at a decent time yourself."

At that, Kellie Jo excused herself, a little embarrassed, and headed back to the cube farm where all the junior agents worked.

Brian refocused on the video screen. "What were those guys—whom I *do* recognize—doing in Northwest Arkansas?" he asked himself.

"Maybe it's time to give Lori another call," Brian thought to himself.

He picked up his phone and dialed Lori.

"Detective Garringer," the voice on the other end answered.

"Hey, Lori," Brian responded.

"Brian?" Detective Garringer asked. "What are you up to on a Saturday morning?"

"Oh, I was just reviewing some information on one of my cases. It reminded me that you never agreed to a drink with me last time you were in town," Brian said in his most southern, charming method.

Even while speaking on the phone, Brian smiled.

Detective Garringer, somewhat giggling, responded, "You are correct. You *do* owe me a drink. You know, I'll be in Fayetteville tomorrow. Maybe we could connect then?"

Brian smiled to himself and reacted, "That's great! Pencil

me in your schedule. By the way, what's bringing you to Fayetteville?"

"Oh, I have something a hiker found that belongs to Megan Ferguson. I just wanted to give it to her, and she is scheduled to be in town."

Brian could feel the adrenaline filling his system. He became incredibly curious.

"Megan Ferguson?" Brian repeated. "Well . . . Jacquelin Vanderli officially now. What did the hiker find?"

"Oh, nothing really. Just a little piece of jewelry that I think belonged to her from years ago."

Brian straightened in his chair. The charm was gone and was replaced by his steely intuition. That intuition had kept him on a promising career path the last few years.

"Why had Lori kept this from him?" he wondered.

"Did you have the crime lab take samples?" Brian finally rallied the voices in his head and responded.

That question seemed to both puzzle and annoy Lori slightly.

"Yes, of course. They are done with their sampling and released it back to me," she answered very diplomatically and officially.

Brian, sensing he maybe sounded inconsiderate, stepped back into his southern, charming self.

"I'm sorry. Of course, you followed the book. Well, then, how about that drink?" Brian summed up with a little light-heartedness.

"Sounds great, Brian," Detective Garringer answered. "I'll see you tomorrow afternoon. Just text me where and when," she completed the conversation.

Chapter 31

Christmas lighting in the downtown square during the evening hours in Fayetteville was one of the prettier sights Jim enjoyed. He was happy to see people embracing a small-town feel the square emitted inside of a more medium-sized town. The square was not only filled with lights, but also provided camel rides, hot cocoa, hot pretzels, cotton candy, and a nightly surprise visit by Santa. He remembered bringing his daughters there when they were younger. Of course, his daughters were older now and had things to do that didn't always include him. Thinking about how pretty the sights were, Jim decided he would go out on a limb and invite Kat.

"How could she turn down a walk through the Fayetteville square?" he mused.

He had been contacting her most days since their near-death experience as the hunted not a week ago. He was only fulfilling his civic duty by keeping her safe, he justified in his head.

But this was different. He felt somewhat like a teenager trying to ask a girl out for the first time. He was nervous and anxious. He called her number and hoped she would not answer so he could just leave the invite on her voicemail . . . but she answered.

"This is Kat," the voice said.

Jim stumbled a little but quickly responded, "Do you like Christmas lights?"

He hit his head with the heel of his hand and decided he should have rehearsed more.

"As a matter of fact, I do," Kat responded.

There was an awkward pause as Jim tried to figure out what to say next; he was not prepared for such a positive response.

"Did you have something in mind?" Kat pressed.

"Well, yes. I was wondering if you would like to go with me to Fayetteville's square. I know that's a little drive, but I have always enjoyed it in the past," Jim heroically summed.

"You know, I have never been to Fayetteville's square in December. I bet it is beautiful. Yes, I would be happy to go," Kat said.

Jim was pleased and somewhat surprised. All he wanted to do was get off the phone.

"Ok . . . tonight . . . maybe meet at the hog at the north end of the square at 8?" Jim suggested.

Kat couldn't help but giggle, "The what?"

"The hog," Jim repeated. "You will understand when you get there."

"It's a date," Kat said.

"10-4" Jim replied and hung up. "10-4?" he repeated to himself as he held his forehead. "Who says stuff like that?"

Promptly at 8 o'clock that night, Jim found Kat standing in front of the "hog." The hog was a large, lit Razorback that many people used as a backdrop for their selfies. She was taking pictures with her cell phone and giggling at the crowd.

He stepped back just to look at her once more before interrupting her fun. Kat stood there, bundled up in a light-blue, fleece coat and matching, knit stocking hat. Her blonde hair flowed over her shoulders. Jim smiled before she saw him. She was clearly enjoying the silly behavior of the young folks and their selfies. Kat's openness in enjoying the simple things in life made Jim feel warm and cheery.

She caught a glimpse of Jim approaching and smiled. He was already smiling, but felt his cheeks burn when he stretched that smile even more. Maybe he was even blushing just a tad.

"I see you found the hog," Jim said, halfway laughing.

Kat laughed at him and responded, "Of course. It seems it is a beacon to the Southeast Conference gods."

Jim laughed with her and thought it a great synopsis. He motioned her to walk with him.

"I am glad you decided to risk being seen in town with a simple guy like me," Jim said.

"Simple?" Kat faulted his word choice. "How can a man who discovers a skeleton and is then hunted be called simple? What kind of world do you live in that that is even common?"

They both chuckled at their strange circumstances.

Jim hated the cold, so he decided hot cocoa was necessary for survival. He offered Kat the same. They were both enjoying what was likely the worst hot cocoa ever consumed by a human but were both genuinely enjoying the moment of newfound friendship.

Jim and Kat continued to walk through the streets, enjoying the people scene. At last, Santa arrived. Jim chuckled at the sight of all the little ones jumping up and down for joy at the sight of Santa.

Kat leaned over to Jim and said, "It won't be long, and we will both enjoy Santa again through the eyes of our grandchildren."

Jim laughed, but hearing the word "grandchildren" reminded him he wasn't that star-struck teenager any longer. He was, instead, a star-struck *middle*-ager.

He took one more glance at Kat's smiling and enjoying the kids and decided, "Who cares?"

Jim slowly slid his hand down from her elbow and gently grabbed her hand. He was astonished at just how little her hand was . . . even dainty.

"Let's get a funnel cake," he said as he pulled her through the crowd in search of the golden brown, latticed pastry.

Kat obliged without any hesitation as a funnel cake sounded tasty. They found their coveted funnel cakes and enjoyed a nice, sugary treat. At that point the realization that they had seen the entire square hit both of them, and they decided to call it a night.

"I hope you had fun," Jim said as he walked Kat to her car.

"I did," Kat responded with yet another smile. "Of course, who wouldn't have fun with you? Running for our lives one minute; grabbing pictures with a giant hog fashioned out of lights the next minute; and then the pinnacle: funnel cakes in the moonlight! You know how to show a girl a good time," she rattled off, laughing intermittingly.

Jim gave her a giant bear hug and tucked her into her car. He watched patiently to make certain her car started, then began his trek towards his truck.

"His truck? Where did he park? Wait . . . where are the keys?"

Chapter 32

Sunday afternoon proved to be another beautiful day. Detective Garringer's drive was great as she drove deep into the countryside on a dirt road toward Kat's house. Detective Garringer had never been to her house before but had been to Huck's cabin and, of course, the cave.

Detective Garringer turned into Kat's drive. She pulled her car up alongside a Nissan Murano with Florida tags. She was certain it was a rental car . . . likely Megan's. Detective Garringer was trained to be observant at all times. At one point, Detective Garringer believed she caught a car following her. As she put her car into park, she watched the road for over a minute to verify. Nothing showed up . . . just her imagination, she concluded.

Detective Garringer grabbed the box and headed to the door. As she got close to the door to knock, Kat opened it.

"You must be Detective Garringer. I would recognize you anywhere from Jim's description."

"Yes Ma'am, I am Detective Garringer. Thank you for allowing me to interrupt your visit," the detective said as she held her badge out for Kat to see.

Over Kat's shoulder she saw a tall, slender, almost old-Hollywood, glam-style lady. Kat welcomed Detective Garringer into the house and introduced her to Megan.

"Megan, this is Detective Garringer," Kat said while showing Detective Garringer into the living room.

Megan, very carefully and with great caution, reached out her hand to greet Detective Garringer.

"It is a pleasure to meet you, Detective. I believe we spoke regarding something from my not-so-distant past," Megan said with very little emotion and great tact.

Detective Garringer held the box out to Megan.

"Kat believes this belongs to you," Detective Garringer said.

Megan looked at the box, then glanced to Kat. By this time, Kat's gleeful face had turned to one of distress and seriousness. She caught Megan looking at her.

Kat nodded, "Yes, Megan, I have seen this box before. Dave showed it to me the day I think he disappeared."

Upon hearing Dave's name, Megan steadied herself and reached for the box. When she opened it, her eyes immediately filled with tears. The tears flowed hard and fast as her hand flew to her mouth. Megan found herself panting for air. Kat rushed over and pulled Megan tightly against her. Megan held onto Kat with everything that was left of her strength. Detective Garringer, realizing that Megan was overcome with emotion, quickly lent a hand to help her to the couch.

"I knew he didn't leave me," Megan repeated over and over.

After many moments of tears, she quickly regained her composure. Detective Garringer, realizing that Megan was in a better state of mind, decided to take the opportunity to ask her a few questions.

"Ms. Ferguson, I'm so sorry to bring all this up again," Detective Garringer started with a strained and concerned face, "but can I ask you some questions about Dave Reid?"

"Yes . . . yes, of course," Megan responded while wiping leftover tears off her cheek.

"What happened on the day Dave disappeared?" Detective Garringer asked. "Please start at the beginning of the day."

"It was like so many other hiking days. Dave asked me to meet him on the bluff. That was kind of our getaway from the world. Back then, Dad didn't approve of Dave . . . said he was just a gold digger. I don't think that's why Dad did not like him . . . but I have never been able to find out the truth.

"Anyway, Dave never showed. After I gave up and came back down from the bluff, I got this text that said something had come up. I remember being so mad," Megan said as she stared numbly into the little box.

She sat, shaking her head from left to right over and over again. Finally, she reclaimed her composure and continued, "I tried calling Dave that night after I got over being mad. He never answered. I was so emotional. I couldn't figure out what was going on. Then the next day arrived . . . no Dave. I tried calling again and again. I told Dad, and he just kept saying that nothing was wrong, that it was election time and Dave was just busy . . . told me to let it go. But I couldn't. I kept calling. Then another day . . . no response from Dave. I called his brother in St. Louis. He said he hadn't heard from him. I finally called his boss, Sofia. She said he had left for Morocco. I knew he had a trip planned. Oddly, that relaxed me a little. But then it was a week . . . no call, no text, no email. I got worried, so I filed a Missing Person Report against Dad's wishes.

"I had a federal agent actually call me to tell me that he could confirm that Dave did, in fact, board a plane to Morocco. The flight manifest had his name on it, and he had reviewed the video footage to confirm a man matching Dave's description did board."

Kat noticed Detective Garringer raising an eyebrow at Megan's memory.

Megan continued, "The agent told me they had no way of knowing what happened to Dave upon arrival at Morocco but felt certain he did leave the United States."

Detective Garringer sat there scribbling something in her notebook.

"I know this is likely impossible but do you remember the agent's name who gave you this information?" Detective Garringer asked.

"No, I'm sorry. I truly cannot remember, and I'm certain I never wrote it down," Megan answered.

"Did the agent think you were his wife . . . or sister?" Detective Garringer asked.

"No, he knew Dave and I were dating and not related. Why?"

"Oh, I'm sure it's just an oversight at the time; but as

agents, we are not allowed to release information to anyone who isn't related to the missing person . . . just protocol."

"I'm sorry I can't be of much help," Megan apologized.

"You've been through a lot," Detective Garringer responded with the greatest empathy.

"Is that Dave's body you found?" Megan timidly asked.

"I cannot confirm just yet, Ms. Ferguson; but yes, I believe it likely is the remains of Dave Reid," Detective Garringer responded.

Kat and Megan both grabbed each other for a long moment. Both women seemed to find strength together.

Megan looked up at Kat and said, "It's finally over."

Megan looked back at the ring in the box. She pulled it out slowly and slid it on her finger. The ring shone and glistened in the light . . . and, of course, it was a perfect fit.

"I would've said 'yes,' you know," Megan said to Kat.

"I know," Kat responded. "You know he loved you," Kat somewhat asked and somewhat stated.

"Yes, I do," Megan responded, almost numbly.

At that moment, Detective Garringer decided she would probably not glean any more new information at this time; so, it was time to leave. She thanked both women for their time and wished them the best. Detective Garringer left the house, climbed into her car, and headed back to Fayetteville to meet Brian for a quick drink.

She arrived at Apple Blossoms in Fayetteville before Brian. Apple Blossoms was one of her favorite little bar and grills . . . always a great atmosphere, good craft beer, and usually a great game on the TVs. The bar at Apple Blossoms was beautiful with deep, mahogany-framed glass shelves on which was displayed every liquor one could imagine. The waitstaff were very prepared and knowledgeable about the in-house craft beers. If one was lucky enough to get the tall kid with a crazy beard, they could receive an education about each and every beer they brewed.

Detective Garringer was being seated when she saw out the window a Lexus drive up that was equally as dirty as her Honda. Detective Garringer remembered thinking she was going to have to wash Kat's dirt road off her car before her trek home. Interestingly enough, it was Brian who stepped out of the Lexus.

"Of course, a Lexus" Detective Garringer whispered to herself while shaking her head.

She settled in and grabbed a drink menu while she waited for Brian to find her. Brian saw her at the bar and waved.

Upon getting closer, he gave Detective Garringer a shoulder hug and said, "Great to see you, Lori."

"Good to see you, Brian," Detective Garringer responded while enjoying the hug. "What have you been up to that your car is so dirty?" Detective Garringer asked with a sarcastic twist.

Brian laughed and responded, "I was just getting ready to ask you the same thing."

They both laughed and ordered beer.

"Of course, with beer one must have the Fayetteweise fries, which are basically a heart attack on fries," Detective Garringer declared to both the waiter and Brian.

"So, did you speak to Megan Ferguson today?" Brian slowly ventured once the waiter left.

"Yes, I did."

"Anything new on the case?" Brian pressed as the waiter abruptly returned with the beverages.

"Nope, not really anything new," Detective Garringer responded while enjoying her first gulp of cold beer.

"Did Megan remember much from those days?" Brian continued yet again.

"No, her only recollections were the day she believes Dave Reid to have gone missing, filing a Missing Person Report, the agent who responded to the Missing Person Report, and . . . well, I guess that's really it," Detective Garringer summed up.

"The agent?" Brian quizzed and smirked.

"Oh, likely a young agent who broke protocol, in my mind. You know how emotional things can get in cases like this. I'm certain it was nothing intentional," Detective Garringer summaried.

"Really? Well, what about . . ." Brian started to ask.

Detective Garringer held up her hand to interrupt him, "Are we gonna talk shop or catch up on *us?*"

They both laughed and Brian agreed to no more shop talk as they dug into the just-arrived, hot fries.

After exiting the bar, Detective Garringer started to get into her car to head back. Brian held the door open for her in true, southern-gentleman fashion but stepped partially in her way, hindering her from actually getting into the car. She glanced up at him questioningly. He leaned forward and gave her the gentlest kiss on her lips. She felt her cheeks burn . . . not out of embarrassment but more out of stimulation.

"Maybe we can grab a drink in the Rock sometime this week or over the weekend," Brian offered as he pulled her close to him. Detective Garringer only responded with a nod and stepped back. He moved out of her way; and she slid into her car, her cheeks still burning.

_____ *Chapter* 33

Detective Garringer arrived at work early on Monday. Although many offices didn't seem to be fully manned until after 8 o'clock in the morning, her office was very different. Many of her peers started the day at 6 a.m. She greeted a young intern as he got off the elevator. By his appearance, she was rather certain he had had a big evening on the town the night before and was trying to cover it today. She laughed to herself and fondly recalled her youth and those days of maturing.

She powered up her laptop. "Fertilizer."

She couldn't get that out of her head. Certainly, Huck wasn't a terrorist. It was hard to believe that he would have anything to do with destruction . . . but there was no doubt that Huck liked to make the mighty dollar.

"How do phosphate trades work?" she whispered to herself.

She Googled "phosphate" and then remembered her conversation with her boss just a couple of days ago.

"Maybe it is better to go old school," she thought.

She needed a phonebook. She glanced at her bookshelf. It had been so long since she used one, she couldn't remember if she even had one in her office. After a quick review, she confirmed her fingers were not going to be able to "do the walking" there.

Detective Garringer looked into the common area at her clerk's desk. Maybe he had one. He was not there just yet, so she decided to go for a quick walk and look through his obvious resources. She didn't agree with going through anyone's desk without their permission.

Detective Garringer stood up and grabbed her coffee cup, deciding to make this trip a "two-fer." As she walked by the clerk's desk, she noticed his pictures. There were several small pictures of his partner, as well as two pug dogs. Detective Garringer couldn't help but grin at the dog photos. It was almost as if those dogs were smiling for the camera.

Ugh, no phonebook in sight.

"And why should there be one? Who uses phonebooks anymore?" she found herself saying out loud.

She wasn't going to give up her hunt that easily. As she walked toward the break room, she glanced at the other clerks' desks . . . nothing in sight. She continued on her way to the break room to grab coffee, which was very much needed at that point. Although the office coffee was good, it certainly paled in comparison to the coffee that she and Jim had been enjoying at their secret meetings. Detective Garringer stopped for a moment, enjoying the caffeine's effects on her brain.

"It is going to be a very long day when the simplest task becomes the most difficult," she thought to herself.

As she moved to leave the break room, she caught a glimpse of a pile of three-ring binders by the copy machine. The three-ring binders were there as a matter of surplus. They had been there for some time as there was a thin layer of dust on them. She had forgotten they were even there . . . and there it was: a glimpse of gold shining through. She reached over and tugged at the golden book. Due to the tower of binders on top, she decided she needed both hands. She placed her coffee mug on the counter and slid the book out from under the leaning tower of plastic.

"Success!" she thought as she checked the tower for any movement.

Granted the date printed on the phonebook said 2011, but it would work. She perused the listings, looking for fertilizer and grain companies . . . any would do. Upon finding a listing, Detective Garringer did a quick glance over each shoulder to see who might be watching her as she continued to impassively sip her coffee.

Verifying she was not being watched, she ripped the needed page out of the phonebook. She folded it and quickly tucked it into her front pants pocket. Swiftly, she replaced the phonebook to its original bedding . . . sorta.

"Good morning, Detective," the voice from behind her boomed.

Detective Garringer, feeling somewhat guilty—of what, she did not know—slowly picked up her mug and spun around to greet her boss.

"Good morning, Captain," she said with a casual grin and took another sip of coffee while keeping her eyes glued on him. "Did you catch the Razorbacks last night?" she continued, knowing he was a huge college basketball fan.

"I sure did! Was a good win for us," the captain said with a chuckle. "We may have a good season."

Detective Garringer took another sip, trying to avoid a conversation, and slid past him through the door, heading to her office. She continued to work through her caseload as it had been piling up on her.

At lunch, she decided to take a quick break. She took the elevator down one floor to the lobby to grab a sandwich. After purchasing her lunch, she pulled the phonebook page out of her pocket. She identified a company that was close enough that she might be able to visit. Now, how to contact them without using her technology . . ..

Her luck seemed to be improving today as in walked one of her casual friends, Lesa, from a law firm down the block. They ran into each other often and had developed a mutually-respectful relationship. As soon as Lesa walked into the building, she noticed Detective Garringer looking at her, so she waved. Detective Garringer motioned for Lesa to come sit with her after she retrieved her meal. Then Detective Garringer picked up her phone and casually turned it off.

Lesa joined her a couple of moments later. They quickly caught up on Lesa's life. She was certainly an interesting character. A single mother, she had worked her way through law school by working for the same law firm that still employed her. Detective Garringer found that incredibly impressive. Currently, Lesa was an attorney and seemed to be getting the green light from her superiors that her future would involve more and more cases.

"Lesa, my phone died just as I entered the sandwich shop," Detective Garringer said as she held up a blank screen. "Would it be possible for me to use your phone for just one call, as I was supposed to call my boss before 1:00?"

"Of course," Lesa responded and started digging in her purse.

After a couple of minutes of mining, Lesa produced an iPhone. Detective Garringer took the phone and excused herself, stepping outside to make her call. Less than two minutes later Detective Garringer returned and handed Lesa her phone.

"Thanks so much for letting me borrow your phone; I hope you didn't miss it much," Detective Garringer laughed with Lesa.

She and Lesa caught up during the remainder of lunch. Detective Garringer enjoyed hearing the shenanigans of Lesa's daughter; but more importantly, she enjoyed watching an animated Lesa tell the stories.

After lunch, Detective Garringer jumped in her car and drove to Newport. A few minutes into her driving, she suddenly became uncomfortable. She remembered she left her phone off. She reached over to the passenger seat, grabbed her phone, and turned it back on.

"Professor Cunningham is contagious," she chuckled to herself.

_____Chapter 34

After a few minutes, Detective Garringer, in deep thought, reached over and turned her phone off again. She pulled up to the Hare Grain Company. Stepping out of her car, she stretched her back, then reached into the back seat for her backpack. She stood facing a tiny brick office that was nestled off the road and to the side of over ten very large grain bins. The area was completely graveled or paved. Behind the giant grain bins were acres of recently harvested corn . . . acres and acres of cropland. Large combines were parked in a neat row to the side. Detective Garringer stood in the parking lot area when a young woman approached her from the office.

"Detective?" the woman inquired.

"Yes, I'm Detective Garringer. I presume you are Jennifer?" Detective Garringer responded while holding out her hand, as well as her badge, to greet the young woman.

"Yes, I am Jennifer. So nice to meet you, Detective. It's not every day a state detective calls, wanting information about phosphate," Jennifer said with a smile and a creased brow as she was clearly confused as to the nature of the visit.

The young woman guided Detective Garringer into the small, brick office. Inside the office were two other private office spaces with a conference-style room in between. It was kept very clean, but there was a small dusting of dirt pretty much everywhere. The young woman ushered Detective Garringer into her office and suggested a seat for her.

"What can I help you with, Detective?" Jennifer questioned.

"I know this is unusual, and I apologize for the late notice. You are very kind to meet with me and help me understand the fertilizer impacts on Arkansas," Detective Garringer responded. "I really just need to understand how fertilizer and, specifically, phosphate can profit in American agriculture."

"Whatever I can do to help," Jennifer politely offered.

"Ms. Hare, let's just start from the beginning as I really know very little about crop production. Help me understand how much phosphate is used in production."

"Certainly," Jennifer said, nodding her head. "It's very interesting that you ask me that question. I serve on the National Grain and Feed Association Board. I have for many years. We started monitoring the supply of nitrogen and phosphate very closely in 2006."

"Why start in 2006?" Detective Garringer quizzed.

Jennifer morphed into professor mode. "Because in 2006 President Bush signed in the Renewable Fuels Standard or RFS Program. That created a large demand on corn as our country started using significant tons of corn for ethanol production. We jumped from 77 million acres planted for corn in 2006 to almost 95 million in 2007. Everyone who could produce corn, did. Corn became very highly demanded as close to 40% of corn is now used for ethanol versus other uses.

"We, as an agricultural unit, were not prepared for that massive growth in that short amount of time. So, fertilizer became a highly demanded product, as well. And, of course, with high demand comes high prices.

"You asked about phosphate. We refer to that as Diammonium Phosphate (DAP). At one point, I think we were spending over $1,200 per ton. To give you a reference, it is now maybe $400 per ton. Those outlandish fertilizer costs continued well into 2010."

Detective Garringer was eagerly and aggressively writing in her notebook.

"So, Jennifer, if someone owned a fertilizer company during 2006-2010, would they have made significant profit?"

Jennifer sat back and thought for a moment.

"Honestly, Detective, I don't think so," she began. "It really would have depended on where the fertilizer companies found their inputs. So, in the case of DAP, where would the fertilizer owner find raw phosphate? Here in the U.S. we were using all we had; so, the input costs would have been high, as well . . . I believe. I think the trick to making money off the fertilizer would have been to find phosphate cheaper than what we, the U.S., could produce."

Detective Garringer quickly scribbled something, then stopped.

"Jennifer, where would you find phosphate outside of the U.S.?"

Jennifer thought for a moment, then responded, "Most of our phosphate imports come from Morocco."

Detective Garringer could feel the blood leaving her face at that moment.

"Did you say Morocco?" Detective Garringer gushed.

"Yes. In fact, the then-Secretary of Agriculture Dobbs had worked hard with the government to improve the processes of importing it. If I remember correctly, Secretary Dobbs was instrumental in relaxing those tariffs in the early years. Since he was elected to governor, I think he has been a good partner for Arkansas agriculture. It seems we have more supply today than ever. He also helps us fight to keep those high-yielding corn species."

Detective Garringer jotted down information in her notepad. The fertilizer business had taken off in 2006. The then-Secretary of Agriculture influenced and aided the import game. Elected to governor, Dobbs continued to influence Congress for tariff and quota improvements. Huck Ferguson started his career of philanthropy in 2009. Dave disappeared in 2010. The governor was elected in 2010. The timeline was tricky but definitely had some suspicious correlations. The real question was what influence did Huck have on Secretary Dobbs, and when did that happen?

Detective Garringer, realizing Jennifer was speaking to her, looked up.

"I'm sorry, Jennifer, I got lost in my train of thought. What were you asking me?" Detective Garringer asked in embarrassment.

"I was asking if you would care for some water; you look parched," Jennifer offered in true southern fashion.

"No, I think I am good. And thank you so very much for your time. I know this was an unusual request."

Detective Garringer stood, shook Jennifer's hand, and gathered her materials. Jennifer walked the detective to her car and wished her well.

Detective Garringer left the Hare Grain Company. She drove three miles, trying to consume all of the details of the case. The details were starting to blend together, yet no real crime was evident.

She swerved into the WalMart parking lot. Once parked, she reached over to retrieve her notebook. She needed to understand the parallel lives of Huck Ferguson and Governor Dobbs. She started a timeline.

1994	*Toby and Mr. Quinn are employed at Carver Wealth Services*
1997	*Toby buys considerable acres in Maumelle, AR*
1999	*SP Industries, LLC, purchases the same land from Toby*
2002	*Toby is appointed to Arkansas Secretary of Agriculture*
2006	*President Bush signs the RFS Act*
2006/7	*Toby actively works to relax the tariffs on goods, specifically phosphate from Morocco*
2008	*Dave Reid starts his job at Sofia Agassi's firm*
2009	*Huck enters the philanthropy world*
2010	*Toby elected to governor*
2010	*Dave visits Morocco*
2010	*Missing Person Report filed, Dave Reid*
2014	*Toby reelected*
2018	*Toby announces presidential run*

Detective Garringer circled the last statement on her timeline.

"Toby . . ." she said. "All roads seem to end at Toby."

She leaned back in her seat, looking out across the parking lot, almost as though she was looking for inspiration.

"What did Dave see in Morocco? And how does that connect to Toby?"

She decided she needed to speak to Jim again. She quickly dug her phone out of her backpack. She realized she had turned it off when she got close to the Hare Grain Company and had forgotten to turn it back on.

"I bet Captain Lambert will be calling me out on this shortly," she whispered to herself.

She started dialing Jim's number, then abruptly stopped. The thought of calling attention to Jim via her phone records concerned her. She did not want to put him at any more risk.

She tapped her fingers on the steering wheel while she brainstormed. Then she had a thought: her radio; his radio. She picked up her phone and went ahead and dialed Jim, as this would be the last time they would communicate via phone.

"This is Jim," the voice on the other end said.

"Channel 3," Detective Garringer responded.

"Channel what?" Jim stuttered; but as he said it, he understood.

They hung up. Jim picked up the radio and adjusted it to channel 3.

"Professor?" Detective Garringer asked.

"Professor is a go," Jim responded.

"I'm sure you understand," Detective Garringer continued.

"10-4 . . . this is a talk-around channel," Jim responded.

"Professor, how do we import minerals from the Sahara?" Detective Garringer asked.

"I'm not an expert; but from what I know, any imports of agricultural goods must be approved by our government and meet our production standards."

Detective Garringer continued to think as she asked, "What standards?"

"There is a purity level and contaminate-free level that has to be audited," Jim responded.

"Audited? Where would the audit take place?" Detective Garringer quizzed as she rubbed her temples. This was all getting so technical.

"At the site of manufacturing," Jim answered. "Oh," he

continued abruptly, "there are also invoicing procedures; currency exchange stuff; and, of course, verification of labor."

"Verification of labor?" Detective Garringer repeated.

"Yes. Of course, all imports into the U.S. have to be approved and audited on their production practices. I am thinking that is the responsibility of the Government of Accountability Office or GAO. At least that's how we go about gaining some of the minerals we use," Jim explained.

"Who is in control of the Accountability Office?" Detective Garringer asked very suspiciously.

"I would have to look that up. Stand by," Jim responded. After a minute of silence, "Detective?" Jim asked.

"Garringer is a go," responded the detective.

"Graham Barnes . . . apparently he has been comptroller general since 2006."

"2006," Detective Garringer said to herself. "10-4, Professor. Out," Detective Garringer ended the communication.

Detective Garringer decided she had avoided Captain Lambert long enough. She started her car and headed back to Little Rock, prepared for a bit of a butt-chewing if he had found out she left her zone without checking out.

_____ Chapter 35

"We need to meet today," the text read.

Sofia stared at her phone. She knew this day would come.

"Happy to oblige, Governor. I understand you are in town. I will send my car for you," she responded.

"No worries. I am on my way. Be there in 5," was the reply.

Sofia tried to mentally prepare for the meeting; this meeting was not about the campaign. At that same moment, she could hear brash laughter in the hallway: Toby was here. He truly had a way of making everyone laugh . . . even chuckle. Without even a knock, he entered her office with a wide smile.

"Sofia! So good to see you," he said and grabbed her up for a giant bear hug.

He released his hug and looked over to her staff, smiled, and waved at them, which was his motion for "leave us alone now." At least his wife wasn't with him, so maybe this conversation would be lighthearted. Toby, without invitation, settled down in one of Sofia's guest chairs.

"So, how was Minnesota?" Sofia started.

"Sofia, listen, you and I both know why I'm here," he started, cutting to the chase. I got a call last week from one of our 'friends' in the Bureau . . . said there was some scuttlebutt around about a young detective from Little Rock nosing around that cold case. Is that true?" Toby asked directly while holding Sofia's gaze long enough to show her who was boss.

"Yes, I also got that same call," Sofia responded.

Toby leaned forward in his chair, placed an elbow on each knee, and held his chin with his right hand.

"I thought we took care of this years ago. What happened?"

Sofia hated these discussions. She loved to support her candidates with the best marketing and campaign ideas. She was known for clever, sneaky solutions. But "this" was not what she wanted in her career . . . not to mention the legal ramifications. Over the years she had convinced herself that since nothing had seemed to come from "this," that it was forgotten and the world was probably better off somehow.

"Toby, this is what I know. At this point, I don't see any evidence of your connection with Dave. I had his work computer checked and replaced. Yes, we found a series of documents that were suspect and would certainly have been damaging. So, I had his home computer seized, checked, and destroyed. But, strangely enough, nothing was on it.

"We had hackers look into his emails. There did seem to be some chatter with a nurse in the Sahara . . . but we couldn't find anything back then or recently that has come from that. We do believe there were copies of those documents made, but we have not found them. That's been about ten years ago. It is unfortunate what happened to Dave. As I understand, it was an accident. Our 'friends' went to confront him and persuade him to move on. There was a struggle. Dave fell. They hid him in the nearest cave. But the problem has reared back up since a government biologist found him, and now there is the potential for this ugly history coming up again."

Sofia paused and took a deep breath.

"Did the detective identify Dave's body?"

Toby looked into Sofia's eyes, leaning back into his chair.

"No, not yet. But I suspect she will today or tomorrow. The coroner's office could delay only so long without raising suspicion."

Sofia looked back at Toby.

"Do you think they can connect this to us?"

Toby chuckled an evil, almost belittling, laugh, "Of course, they can! We just have to make certain they don't." Toby stood up and bent over the desk to look Sofia directly in the eyes as he instructed her, "Contact Ben . . . *yet again*. Tell him to clean this up . . . *yet again*. But *this* time, no evidence left behind! And to be on the safe side, you should probably call Graham."

After that, Toby straightened up, buttoned his suit coat,

and in a loud voice for the benefit of those on the other side of her door said, "Thanks again, Sofia, for all your support."

He turned, winked at Sofia, and opened the door.

"I've got an election to go win," he boomed as he walked toward the hallway past a group of smiling people in true political fashion. Sofia followed Toby only as far as her office door, smiling in true campaign manager fashion, as well. The campaign must go on.

She turned back into her office, shutting the door. She walked quickly over to her phone.

"SP Industries," the voice on the other end said.

"Could I leave a message for Ben, please?" Sofia inquired.

"Certainly," the receptionist responded.

"Please have Ben call Sofia; he knows my number."

"Of course," the very skilled receptionist replied.

Sofia hung up the phone and waited for the call. She knew it would only be a couple of minutes . . . and she was right: the phone rang barely two minutes later. Sofia picked up the phone and dropped her normal, tactful self.

"He was just here. He told me to connect with you. It needs to disappear," she cryptically said.

"I handle it *personally* this time," Ben responded in broken English and with a heavy accent.

"Out of curiosity, were you able to locate the thumbdrive?" Sofia asked.

"Not yet. I had men look. We no found it at the site. One man watch the biologist's house. We don't think he know what he has. But we will find it and all our problems disappear," Ben brokenly concluded.

After Sofia put things into motion with Ben, she decided she needed to call Graham as Toby requested. She had discovered that working with Graham was exhilarating at first. He had the money, the influence, and the right ideas to improve the country. However, he had no tact; he developed enemies. He clearly was not a man of integrity. Graham was out to win at all costs.

When Toby was first "selected" by Graham to be the next president, Sofia was invited to attend an endorsement meeting at his Heritage Group. The meeting was held in Virginia at some country club called "The Dominion," a nickname for the state from Revolutionary days. Graham's closest friends were there . . . all men of means and influence. Sofia had never felt more uncomfortable in her life; but because of her close relationship with Toby, she was allowed to attend.

Sofia, a veteran of campaigns, thought she had found a creative means to raise funds or at least how to put pressure on people and groups to convince them of their new loyalty to the better candidate. With the latest pressures of campaigning and new campaigning laws, the special interests, such as the Heritage Group, found it difficult to remain invisible. However, *these* people were clever . . . cleverer than she had ever seen.

Utilizing an international commodity to raise funds in a foreign subsidiary was brilliant . . . not only brilliant, but they had anticipated this move for almost a decade. Toby had been hand-selected and groomed years earlier for this moment. First this group assisted him in his cabinet appointment to Secretary of Agriculture for Arkansas. During the meeting, they laughed and joked about getting him that first appointment, which was needed so he could influence policies and the recipient businesses, who later became large PAC donors. Then they got him elected to governor—years in the making.

While Sofia quietly took that meeting in, she realized there was no way out. She had to get Toby elected. Nothing could stand in her way . . . not to mention what she and Graham did ten years before to keep their candidate safe. Today, she had to call Graham once again regarding that event ten years ago.

"Graham. What do you want?" was the gruff answer.

"Graham, Sofia. Toby asked me to check in," Sofia responded in a dull, somewhat repelled, tone. "There seems to have been a discovery in Cherokee City a month ago."

"Has it hit the media?" Graham inquired.

"No. No concrete information has actually been discovered. So far, only a body . . . nothing identifying him. And before you ask, no information was found on or near the body. I have a man already in motion to put a lid on this once and for all," Sofia quickly rattled off in one hurried breath.

"Good! It is ridiculous that this has come up again. If this crap gets out, I will be ruined; and our plans for a decade will be shot to hell!" Graham exclaimed. "Is Toby holding up? Do I need to be worried about him?"

Sofia shook her head to herself before speaking. "No need to worry about Toby, Graham. He is a rock. He totally understands the implications of this find. Like I said, I've got a man on it. In a couple of days this will fade completely away before anyone realizes any connections."

"Good, good!" Graham said loudly and proudly. "We are on the brink of the party nomination. We can't have a media frenzy now."

Graham took a long, loud breath and then stated in a low, completely sinister tone, "Sofia, if you think this is going to get away from us, let's activate our Plan B. We still have time to get her the party nomination if we have to."

"Understood," Sofia responded. "But I assure you, this is just a hiccup and bad luck. I just wanted to make certain you were in the loop."

With that last note from Sofia, Graham hung up without

another word. Sofia stretched her back as she had managed to slouch forward under the stress of the call.

"Plan B can *never* be an option, Graham," she said to herself.

Chapter 37

After Detective Garringer's radio call, Jim started thinking about minerals . . . minerals from the Sahara. He had done some research into harmful minerals in Arkansas streams.

"Where was that material?" Jim whispered to himself.

He started surveying his filing cabinets. He pulled out drawer after drawer. During his search, he found an old birthday card his youngest daughter had given him years ago when she was something like 11 years old. He chuckled at her handwriting. He also found a performance review he apparently never completed or delivered.

"No matter; that guy quit," Jim said toward the paper as a bit of justification as he crumpled it and tossed it on the floor.

He found an interesting pile that seemed to fit the bill. He started digging through the papers. The papers were reports that reflected several minerals and their impact to Arkansas streams. He started reviewing the old data. Obviously, nitrogen had been the common criminal, but phosphorus had certainly contributed to watershed problems. And phosphate had been heavily imported for years.

He suddenly seemed to recall attending a talk at one of the Arkansas Game and Fish Conventions years ago.

"Tristan?" Jim shouted down the office hallway.

"Yeah?" Tristan hollered back.

"Do you remember our attending a talk about phosphate years ago when we were in Atlantic City?" Jim asked as he started walking towards Tristan's little office area.

"Area" would be the best description of where Tristan worked. A young man in his early 30s, Jim found him buried under cables, wires, nets, and towers of paper. He was a man who loved to be outside; so, to his best effort, he avoided the inside . . . and it was obvious.

"Yeah, Jim, I do remember. Some nurse was presenting. If I remember, she was a cute thing. I think I even remembered commenting at the time how hot she was," Tristan said while looking forward, reminiscing.

Jim nodded his head in agreement and was about to ask more questions when Tristan interrupted, "You know, she was *really* hot . . . kinda reminded me of your oldest daughter."

Jim grimaced at hearing a man refer to his daughter as "hot."

He shook off the comment and continued, "Do you remember what her plight was?"

Tristan, sitting in the middle of the floor covered in parts and wires, put everything down and concentrated.

"Something about humanity issues in the Sahara. I think we were included because of the mines, which produce some of the minerals we use."

Jim tried to remember, again rubbing the stubble on his face.

Tristan popped up with a eureka moment, "You know, I think we all donated some money that day. Come to think of it, I don't think I ever deducted that donation."

Jim watched as Tristan's mind worked. He was brilliant but as absent-minded as anyone he had ever met.

"Thanks, Tristan," Jim said as he started to exit the room. He suddenly stopped and looked over his shoulder at Tristan, "By the way, Tristan, stay away from my daughter."

Tristan looked up confused and laughed a little, never fully understanding Jim's point.

Jim returned to his desk and Googled "Morocco mines." To his surprise, several articles listed in his search. Several of those articles were written on the basis of the abuse of workers in the mines. Jim glanced through the articles to see notes of calls for help to the U.S. Government of Accountability Office.

"Why would our government ignore their pleas for help?" Jim thought to himself.

Being cynical, Jim continued with his thought, "Unless somebody in our government is making money. Maybe I should do some digging into our government watchdog herself," Jim muttered as he picked up his phone and started scrolling for a name and number. "Ah ha," Jim announced as he found the name for which he was looking.

Tracy Belcher was a veteran of the Environmental Protection Agency (EPA). She managed the communication sector for the agency. She was very involved in publicizing research and more or less worked as a public relations officer. In that capacity, she constantly sent Jim papers for comment as was their policy to get their papers published. He had befriended her years ago when she sought some assistance getting enough information together to support a congressional bill that the EPA was proposing.

"Tracy Belcher," the voice said.

"Tracy, how goes the good fight?" Jim teased.

Tracy laughed and responded as she recognized the voice, "Mr. Cunningham, it goes with or without me in it. How the heck are you?"

Jim returned the chuckle, "Listen, Tracy, I'm calling you for personal reasons; and honestly, I need you to keep this between you and me."

"Not a problem," Tracy responded confidently and seriously. "What can I do for you?"

"Can you tell me anything about Graham Barnes at the GAO?"

Tracy seemed taken aback, certainly because this question was not what she was expecting.

"Well, anything specific about Graham?" she prodded.

"Nope, I'm just curious about his credibility, his integrity... that kind of thing."

"I see. Well, Jim, off the record I will tell you he is just another one of them. I mean, he is a true politician. He very much stays under the radar, but I can tell you from my experience he seems to have a lot of the brightest and best going in and out of his office. As far as our world, he seems to be incredibly influential. Anything more specific that I can help you with?" Tracy inquired.

"Tracy, is he a by-the-book kind of guy?"

"No. No, Jim, he is not. He seems to stay clean, but he also seems to be in the shadows of a lot of rumor. But he is smart. He is that guy who rides the right shirttails," Tracy answered with caution.

"Have you heard anything about falsifying international audits to keep a flow of goods?" Jim asked more specifically as he gained confidence in Tracy's willingness to keep a secret.

"That's a pretty serious statement, Jim, as Graham's entire purpose for being is to *ensure* credibility in those international transactions. With that being said, I have never seen anything or heard of anything specific, but there were rumors . . . maybe five years ago . . . that he was making a lot of unannounced trips to the Sahara. Some of those trips were even with your governor. The general vibe here was that it is possible they were going to crack down on some of the product from that area. Then there was some blowup with the WHO while they were there . . . something about violations to humanitarian efforts. But they came back, and I guess all was improved. Nothing more was said," Tracy summed up.

"Jim, I think if you need more specific information regarding the activity of the GAO, I would recommend you speak to Donna Mitchell. She is a former Senator from Wisconsin. I trust her . . . and I trust very few people here. She seems to be a straight shooter. I recommend her because she served on the Environment and Public Works Committee in Congress. From what I can tell, she had some run-ins with Graham. She will likely be able to give you better understanding to whatever it is that you are chasing. I'll text you her personal cell number."

"Thanks, Tracy. I appreciate your info. I just had a colleague who had some questions about Graham, and I knew you would have a better and more thorough opinion of him than I could have. Again, I would appreciate we keep our conversation between us," Jim said.

"Anytime, Jim . . . but since I have you on the phone, you owe me comments on the paper about trout stocking numbers in Arkansas streams. We plan to go to press with that in less than a month," Tracy chastised him.

"Yes, Ma'am. You will have those comments tomorrow. Thanks, again," Jim said and hung up while cringing at the fact he had forgotten to complete the paper.

Jim started the search for the paper he knew he had printed and started to review. He moved piles and piles of paper, searching. His office was not much more organized than Tristan's. He then moved to the tops of the filing cabinets. Those papers were "to be filed" any day now. But again, he found nothing.

He stuck his head out his door and asked his secretary, "Have you seen those papers from the EPA research from last week?"

His secretary shook her head in disappointment.

"Have you looked in your briefcase?" she asked as the idea popped into her head.

A look of defeat and embarrassment came over Jim's face. Of course, she had printed it out for him a few days ago; and he had stuck it in his briefcase on his way out of the office. After seeing the look on his face, his secretary smiled a vindicated smile.

Jim walked back into his office, opened up his briefcase . . . and there on top was the elusive paper on which he needed to comment. Not only was the paper there, but there was also his water bill . . . which was now overdue.

"Ugh," Jim uttered while shaking his head.

"I'm going to the water authority building and home from there," Jim said to his secretary on his way out the door. "I'll finish up the paper from home."

His secretary gave him a nod and spun back around to her computer.

"Gonna be a *long* night," Jim thought to himself.

Chapter 38

Jim decided to give former Senator Donna Mitchell a quick call on his way to the water authority to pay the forgotten bill. Fully expecting to be sent to her voicemail, he quickly caved to the urge for caffeine; so, he pulled through Sonic at the same time.

Just as the attendant responded to Jim's order request, Donna Mitchell answered the phone, "This is Donna," the voice said.

"Sir, did you say you want diet Coke easy on ice?" the Sonic attendant asked.

Jim, now in a predicament, as two people—neither of whom were in front of him—were expecting an answer.

"Um . . . yes, diet Coke, please . . . and Ms. Mitchell, my apologies. I was fully expecting your voicemail," Jim stumbled through.

"Ha! No problem. How can I help you?" she asked.

"Ms. Mitchell, my name is Jim Cunningham. I am friends with Tracy Belcher. She recommended I speak to you about some research I am performing."

"That will be one dollar, ten cents," the young woman at his window said.

"Excuse me, Ms. Mitchell," Jim said as he hurriedly explored his truck for change. He managed to find the change but dropped it twice before he could get it out of the window to the carhop. He could hear Ms. Mitchell chuckle slightly as he was certain she heard everything. After finally getting his drink squared away, he returned his attention to the call at hand.

"My apologies, again, Ms. Mitchell. I know you are a very busy woman, so I'm a little embarrassed," Jim, being overwhelmed, confessed.

"Mr. Cunningham, I don't mind at all. Honestly, a little reality is a great haven for me at the moment," she responded lightheartedly. "And if you are a friend of Tracy's, then I hold you in the highest regard. What can I do for you?" she asked again.

"Ms. Mitchell, I am curious about a man named Graham Barnes. He seems to have some strong ties to a couple of people here in Arkansas. And to be blunt, I'm just seeking information on his credibility," Jim stated.

"Ah, I see," Ms. Mitchell said thoughtfully. "Mr. Cunningham, I am assuming since you are calling me and checking Graham's credibility, the ties he has in Arkansas may not be, let's say, ethically superior ties. Would that be correct?" she prompted.

Jim was a bit on-the-spot now as the former Senator seemed to be spot-on with her question. Now was the time to fish or cut bait for Jim. He had to tell her something.

"Yes, his ties may have some friends and colleagues of mine possibly wrapped up into . . . let's say, less than legal . . . activities," Jim stated in what almost seemed an out-of-body experience.

"I see. Yes, Graham is definitely a man who would push any legal or ethical boundaries. I've known him for close to 20 years. We had some volatile interactions maybe four years ago while I served on a committee in Congress. Is there something specific you are searching for?"

"No, I really don't know the specifics at the moment; and to be honest, I'm a little hesitant to share what little I do know," Jim replied.

"No problem," Ms. Mitchell continued. "I'll give you what history I know about him and maybe that will answer your questions. Graham is from Virginia . . . and he is very proud of being from Virginia. He is quite the history buff . . . which is great. He understands the Declaration of Independence and the Constitution likely better than most Supreme Court justices. But Graham has an ego . . . a *very large* ego. He makes it a habit to give these little gifts relating to Virginia to his friends and his enemies—you know, like dogwood stuff, little replicas of Thomas Jefferson, anything that says 'Old Dominion' as is the nickname for Virginia. I know that sounds strange. I am convinced this is his way of reminding people that he is always watching.

"Anyway, he was appointed to comptroller, also known as the Director of the GAO. People don't think much about the appointment, but it is one of the more powerful and least understood positions. Did you know a comptroller is appointed for *15 years?*" Ms. Mitchell asked.

"Um . . . no. I didn't even really know what the head dog *title* was, let alone for how long he would be that head dog," Jim responded.

Ms. Mitchell laughed and continued, "Yes, for *15 years*. I'm not completely certain, but I'm thinking he was confirmed in 2006. So, he will be here for a while longer.

"Anyway, the personal side of Graham is quite enigmatic. He belongs to some kind of heritage society that performs some kind of watch dog function in case our country goes astray from the Constitution. It is top-secret. Nobody has been able to verify that. The intent doesn't sound too bad, but why keep that a secret?

"Anyway, he has successfully offended the entire female population on The Hill, me included. But somehow, he seems to escape any disciplinary action. He was rumored to have been involved in a money laundering attempt in his early 30s before politics consumed him. But those charges were dropped due to lack of evidence . . . or so they say. I will say the latest rumor is that he is guilty of tampering with some trade policies to financially benefit someone. I don't know who is on to him, but this rumor is gaining some traction. I have to admit, not two months ago I tried to find out more information regarding the trade policy violations but came up short."

"Could those violations regard drugs or agricultural commodities?" Jim asked.

A bit of silence pursued as he heard a tapping on the other end, as though Ms. Mitchell was tapping either her pencil or fingernail.

"You know, it really could have been. There are so many rules of international trade that, regardless the product, even a slight variation to policy could make someone rich or someone poor. I'm guessing whatever variation he concocted found some friend of his mighty happy.

"He is smart, Mr. Cunningham. I doubt he would ever take possession of 'found funds.' But he would definitely use those funds to aid him through favors down the road," she summed.

"Ms. Mitchell, I thank you very much for your assistance. One more question . . ." Jim drug out. "What would motivate someone who seems to study and know the Constitution to back a presidential candidate?"

"Well, the Supreme Court justices," she quickly and very confidently responded. "The next president will likely nominate at least two, if not three, justices. Someone like Graham would want to influence those nominations to secure a political fortress around the Constitution."

Jim took a deep breath.

"Of course," he thought, "the justices are a *lifetime* appointment. What better way to preserve your definition of 'heritage'?"

"Thank you, Ms. Mitchell. You have been incredibly helpful. I'm sorry to have interrupted your day," Jim thanked her politely.

"Of course. Anytime. Thank you for reaching out. Mr. Cunningham, please feel free to call me anytime. And I must ask, if you find any information that may impact Graham, would you do me a favor and call me? I am always eager to . . . let's say . . . promote an opponent," she said as she giggled almost sinisterly.

Jim laughed, as well, and hung up. Taking a big sip of diet Coke, he reflected on his gut feeling: Graham was not to be trusted, and there was something going on here in Arkansas that was tied to the White House . . . there was no doubt!

Chapter 39

Detective Garringer spent most of the night tossing and turning. She became increasingly concerned about the concept of phosphate imports coming into the United States from some guy named Bin Moussa, according to Brian at the Bureau. Even more concerning was who was calling the shots, and would that be the same one responsible for Dave's death and—maybe even worse—planning on more deaths?

She finally gave up her quest for sleep and started reading through her old notes and looking through the internet for more information. At 1 a.m., she was reading more about Governor Dobbs' election when she noticed that Sofia Agassi would be making an appearance at a rally later that day in Little Rock. Detective Garringer decided that was opportunity knocking.

She finally chose to exit her bed a little later that morning despite her lack of sleep. She called in to Captain Lambert and told him she was not feeling well. She quickly showered, dressed, and headed down to her car. She drove to the location of the rally, a large stadium downtown. It certainly was busy for being so early in the day.

Detective Garringer guessed that Sofia would be in the middle of the arrangements, because she was the type who did not like surprises. Detective Garringer noticed a lady in the distance who must be Sofia. She was correct: Sofia was dressed in a gray pantsuit with a portfolio in one hand, cell phone in the other.

Detective Garringer heard Sofia ask, "The security staff will be on the premises at what time? Good! And, just to confirm, how many guards will be patrolling in the stands? Good! Good!"

Detective Garringer made her way through the stadium to talk to Sofia. Twice, a staffer or security guard approached her. She simply presented her badge and was always allowed further entry. Soon, the detective stood directly in front of Sofia.

She held out her badge and said, "Sofia Agassi? I am Detective Garringer; would you have a moment for a couple of questions?"

Sofia almost seemed relieved to hear Detective Garringer introduce herself . . . almost as though she anticipated the confrontation and, finally, it was here.

"Of course, Detective. What can I help you with?" Sofia responded as she gently pulled Detective Garringer by the elbow to another location away from earshot of the others.

"Thank you, Ms. Agassi. I know you are busy so I will be brief," Detective Garringer responded. "I am following up on a cold case involving Dave Reid. I understand he used to work for you?"

"Yes, Dave did work for me many years ago. Have you found him?" Sofia asked in what Detective Garringer determined to be fake excitement.

"Possibly. What was Dave's role in your company?"

"He was one of my analysts. He helped to research data for my candidates. He was certainly one of the best I have ever seen," Sofia continued.

"Can you tell me why you had an analyst travel to Morocco?" Detective Garringer continued as she made notes, making the inquisition seem quite official.

"Of course. Dave was accompanying a candidate who had significant ties both to the international and local commodity trading world," Sofia responded bluntly and shortly.

"What candidate?"

Beginning to appear very uncomfortable, Sofia answered, "At the time, Secretary Dobbs. He was running for Governor of Arkansas. Detective, I believe all of this information can be found in my original statement to the police when Dave's Missing Person Report was filed. Did you bother to read that?"

Detective Garringer realized she had hit a nerve, gave a quick grin, and nodded, "Yes, Ma'am, I did read your statement. I am just doing some follow-up. Only a couple more questions. Why did Dave make several return trips to Morocco?"

"I am not certain. I only sent him twice: once with Secretary Dobbs and a second time to get some follow-up statements from the businesses and people of that area. Any other possible trips were on his time and dime," Sofia continued as she crossed her arms and stared up at Detective Garringer.

"I see," Detective Garringer said as she noted something in her notebook. "And do you know a Bin Mousa?"

Detective Garringer watched casually to see Sofia's reaction. Sofia stiffened even more . . . exactly what Detective Garringer anticipated.

"No," Sofia simply answered.

"I see," Detective Garringer continued. "Do you know if Bin Mousa and Governor Dobbs have any business dealings with each other?"

At this point, Sofia became visibly irritated yet tried to control her emotions as she knew she might be a suspect.

"I am unaware of Governor Dobbs' business relationships. That is a better question for him. I will be happy to try to work you in for a quick conversation, maybe after the election," Sofia responded curtly.

"I understand. With Governor Dobbs being your candidate, I would think you might have more intimate knowledge of his business practices. It seems Governor Dobbs and Huck Ferguson have had many years of trades with a Bin Mousa," Detective Garringer tactfully responded, realizing she was getting closer to the truth.

"I don't know a Bin Mousa. I don't know if Governor Dobbs knows a Bin Mousa. Do you have any proof that the two of them have any semblance of a business relationship? If so, I would like to see it, please," Sofia very carefully selected her words.

"Of course, you would. I'll be in touch, Ms. Agassi," Detective Garringer summed.

She walked out of the stadium, having found the answers she needed.

Sofia eyed the detective as she exited the stadium before quickly punching in numbers on her phone.

Again, a very-abled receptionist answered, "SP Industries. How may I help you?"

"Please have Ben call Sofia," Sofia demanded and immediately hung up the phone without waiting for a reply.

A minute later her phone rang.

"The detective was just here. She knows about you and Toby. I don't know how, but she knows," Sofia blurted.

"It's not possible for her to have any information . . . unless that biologist found something. I'll put a man on it immediately. Sofia, don't worry. I'll take care of this," Ben replied.

Sofia hung up the phone and decided to make one more call. She needed to cover all the bases.

"Pinick," the voice on the other end said.

"Brian, a detective was just here. She has pieced together a connection between Toby and Ben. Make it go away if you want this arrangement to continue," Sofia said.

"Done," was all that Brian said as he hung up the phone.

Chapter 40

The sun challenged Jim to get up. The warm rays coaxed his eyelids open. Jim decided to fight it for another few minutes of sleep. However, Jax had a better idea: Jim heard Jax scratch at their back door. Apparently, Jim wasn't moving fast enough so Jax jumped up on Jim's bed and started the stare-down. Jim felt the weight of his trusty companion and decided he was overruled for more sleep.

Jim put both feet on the floor and walked to the back door. He opened it and let Jax out, waiting for him to do his business while slipping on a pair of jeans and a sweatshirt. Looking out at the beautiful morning, Jim decided it was time to step out into a wonderful, albeit unusually warm, nearly January day.

Jim's cabin sat in a secluded, wooded spot on Beaver Lake. This had become his sanctuary. His three neighbors all seemed to have the same goal for living there: privacy.

His cabin was small, two bedrooms and one bathroom . . . definitely decorated for a man, which meant sparsely and rustic, a work in progress. Jim's kitchen was the one area that stood out as odd. Although a small kitchen, it housed the best of appliances. One of Jim's guilty pleasures was cooking. He enjoyed creating his next masterpiece, but often created the next feast for the raccoons outside.

Jim exited the cabin and headed to his shop situated at the end of a small walkway. Parked outside of the shop was an old boat. The boat had seen better days. It looked as though Jim was in the process of performing an autopsy on the motor with wires running in every direction.

The boat's purpose was that of a shocker boat. The boat would skid through low water and shock the fish, leaving them temporarily stunned. In protective suits, the biologists would walk alongside the boat, sample the fish, record the data, and then release the fish back into their environment.

The reason the boat was parked today and being modified was that the shocker system wasn't working well. In fact, the last voyage rendered Jim shocked so much that he fidgeted for two days with tremors. He was certainly not going to let that happen again . . . unless Tristan wanted to take it out. Of course, there was the recent initiation of a young tech working for Jim. Inevitably, newbies who walked the water would grab the metal boat accidentally out of habit . . . always good for a laugh.

Jim was checking the voltage surge in one of the wires when he heard Jax growl . . . such an unusual sound from him.

"Jax, you chasing a groundhog?" Jim called over his shoulder.

Jax barked. The bark sent an alert through Jim. He had heard that sound only once before. He carefully slid his hand towards his pocket to check for his concealed weapon. Of course, it was not there . . . again. But fortune was on his side today as he saw his shotgun still leaning against the shop door after an issue with a raccoon just last week.

Jim turned around to discover a man entering the yard but at bay by Jax.

"Hello there," the man shouted and waved.

"Jax, come here," Jim commanded.

"So sorry to have upset Pooch there," the man said and extended his hand for a shake. "I'm Richard."

Jim mutually extended his hand, "Good morning, Richard. Jim."

Noticing Jim's caution, Richard quickly spoke up, "I was out here walking around a small lot I'm considering purchasing. It's certainly beautiful out here, isn't it?"

Jim relaxed a little after hearing the man's explanation for his presence.

"Good to meet you, Almost Neighbor," Jim said with a

goofy smile. "Yes, it is beautiful . . . one of the most relaxing places on Earth."

"Right. How long have you lived here?" Richard inquired.

"Only about three years . . . after my liberation from my ex-wife," Jim joked.

Richard caught the joke and chuckled.

"Do you hike these areas?" Richard continued his inquiry.

"Some. I'm one of the lucky ones who gets to explore for a living, so I don't hit this area as much as I should," Jim replied.

"Oh, really? Any other interesting spots to explore around here . . . or even a little way out? I love to hike," Richard added.

Jim covertly looked Richard over. He noted that Richard looked like he had just stepped out of an L.L. Bean catalog. His cargo pants and shoes looked brand new.

As Jim continued tugging on the boat's motor wires, he answered, "Oh, you can find some great trails around Devil's Den about 45 miles south of here." Jim kept his tone in educator mode.

"That's great . . . but I was thinking of some trails off the beaten path. I've heard there are some good caves to explore," Richard continued to prod.

"Caves," Jim thought. "That is pretty specific," he said as he kept his eyes on the work at hand.

Jim stood up, wiping his hands on a rag. He looked directly at Richard.

"Where did you say you were from, Richard?" Jim questioned.

Richard, sensing Jim's newfound caution, started to fidget. Jim, likewise, noticed the resulting change in Richard's demeanor. The two stood quietly and awkwardly, staring suspiciously at each other. Jim became very uneasy . . . wishing he had that gun closer.

Richard finally broke the silence, "Well I think I have worn out my welcome. I better head back to the realtor's office before she goes home."

Jim nodded and carefully watched Richard exit the yard. Jax, who was standing next to Jim the entire time, was still on guard. Jim reached down and patted him.

"Good boy! Let's keep an eye out for creepy Richard," he whispered to his pal.

Jim stepped over to his truck, picked up his radio, and confirmed channel 3.

"Detective Garringer," he said and awaited her response. After a minute, he tried her again, "Detective Garringer."

"Detective Garringer a go," he finally heard.

"Jax and I just had a visit from someone here at my home, wanting to know where good hiking in northwest Arkansas could be found . . . specifically, caves."

"Oh, really?" Detective Garringer responded. "What happened?"

"Not a lot," Jim continued. "Jax kinda scared him away, but I am telling you he was looking for information, and I'm certain he was scoping my place out," Jim added.

"Professor, be on the lookout. I'm sorry that I have drug you into this, but it seems we have uncovered something. I'm just not completely sure what that is yet."

"10-4" Jim responded.

Chapter 41

Jim continued to work on his boat but couldn't get the image of creepy Richard, who had invaded his and Jax's yard this morning, out of his head. It occurred to Jim that there had been some unusual happenings since the day he and Jax were hunted only three weeks ago.

He and Detective Garringer had discovered, what he believed, was the true identity of the body. Detective Garringer had contacted him to report that there might be a strange connection between the body and the Sahara and phosphate. In Jim's mind, there were only two uses for phosphate: fertilizer and explosives . . . then, not to forget, creepy Richard from this morning.

He was struggling to loosen a bolt on the boat motor when the wrench popped off the nut, flinging his hand into the metal casing of the motor.

"Damn!" Jim cursed in pain. While he was rubbing his wounded hand, it occurred to Jim, "If someone has tracked me down and assumes I have knowledge of a crime, then they very well could track Kat down."

Jim trotted into his cabin. He came back out with not only his trusty handgun that he never remembered, but he also had grabbed his shotgun from the shop door.

"Load up, Jax," Jim commanded as he held the truck door. "We are going on a rescue mission."

Jim drove speedily out of his driveway and started trying to call Kat on his cell phone. There was no answer. After several calls remained silent, Jim radioed Detective Garringer.

"Detective Garringer?"

"Garringer is a go."

"Hey, this may be nothing, but I have been trying to reach Kat for the last 20 minutes and can't reach her. Do you think maybe you could send a patrol car out to her place . . . just to make certain she is okay? I'm on my way there now."

"Done," replied Detective Garringer.

Jim arrived at Kat's cottage another 15 minutes after his call. There was no patrol car in the driveway. He didn't see any signs of Kat on the front porch. Jim grabbed his shotgun, jumped up on the porch, and knocked on the door, this time carefully stepping to one side and very much on alert. There was nothing from inside. Jim knocked again and checked the doorknob. The door was unlocked. He carefully opened the door and crept into Kat's house, shotgun at the ready. Jax absentmindedly followed.

"Kat?" Jim shouted. "You in here?"

There was no response. He checked every room to no avail. Kat was not in the unlocked house. He picked up his phone to call Detective Garringer when he heard something from the back porch. Gun poised, he cautiously stepped through the kitchen to try to discover the origin of the sound.

Standing on the back porch was Kat, removing her coat and muck boots. As she opened the porch door to enter the kitchen, she saw Jim standing across from her, gun in hand. She instinctively jumped backward, letting the door slam shut, and let out a little scream before she fully recognized Jim. Upon the realization that Jim was the one standing in front of her, she bent over, placing her hands on her knees, and gave short, little pants to catch her breath.

"What the hell are you doing?" she asked painfully between each breath.

"I was worried you might be in trouble," Jim responded.

"So, you decided to kill me by way of a heart attack?" Kat replied as she stood up and placed a hand on her chest.

Kat lit up a small smile. Jim was happy to see that she was smiling and that it seemed she would survive.

"I had an incident at my house earlier today with a possible intruder. I called you to warn you, but you didn't answer. I became worried that said intruder may be coming your way. I thought it best if Jax and I came to rescue you, as we were certain you were a damsel in distress," Jim kiddingly continued.

Kat's eyes narrowed at his perception of her possibly being a damsel in distress. She then walked toward her back door and made a second attempt to enter her kitchen.

"I was out hiking. Tell me more about your intruder and why your enemies would want to inflict any harm on *me*," Kat said semi-jokingly.

"Kat—by the way, you look great today," Jim flirted, hoping a little compliment might get him out of trouble with her. "Seriously, though, the cold case possibly involving Dave Reid is getting stranger. I am beginning to think the men hunting me a few weeks ago were actually trying to locate something, and I just happened to stumble into the area . . . or worse: maybe thinking I had actually located something. Kat, I truly don't want to distress you anymore than nearly killing you already; but I do believe the skeleton we found in Huck's cave is that of Dave Reid and that he knew something on someone."

Kat stood motionless. Jim was convinced she would break down in tears hearing the skeleton was likely Dave Reid's. Instead, she was clearly processing the information.

"I know," she finally said. "I know that is Dave's remains."

Jim was shocked to hear Kat's surrender to what appeared to be the truth.

Kat continued, "It is just too coincidental that he was never heard from again. There is no way he would've stood up Megan. The morning that I last saw him . . . he was a boy in love. He wouldn't have left her. I have known that for a while. I've had no evidence . . . and truly, still don't. But I have feared Huck had something to do with his disappearance."

Kat moved over to the couch and sat down, seemingly defeated. Jim unloaded his gun and leaned it against the wall. He carefully and slowly moved to a seat on the couch next to Kat.

Kat continued speaking in a low voice, "Dave was such an energetic and smart boy. I feared he had uncovered something working for that woman in St. Louis. She is in politics; and let's face it, the only people who succeed in politics are criminals. I remember Dave telling me stories about all the influential people he had met. Then, something changed in his demeanor. He became callous . . . almost cynical when it came to his work."

Kat leaned into Jim as she reminisced. Jim certainly listened to everything Kat said but was getting lost in her fragrance. Those blue eyes that so entranced him looked up into his and caught him off guard.

"Is that what you think?" Kat repeated.

Jim was caught; he overestimated his ability to listen and look.

His bumfuzzled look prompted Kat to repeat a third time, "Do you think Huck killed Dave?"

Jim, snapping back to reality, sat there, contemplating for a moment . . . a long moment as he collected his thoughts.

Finally, he responded as he stared into her blue eyes once again, "Kat, I'm not a detective. I'm a simple biologist who loves nature amongst other things. But what doesn't seem to add up to me is, if I were going to kill someone, why would I dispose of their body on my own property? That kinda seems to be damning evidence."

Kat shook her head, almost relieved, "I've thought the same thing."

Chapter 42

Overcome by emotion, Kat reached over and buried her face in Jim's chest and started taking deep breaths. Jim noticed she was trembling slightly at first, but the trembles eased quickly . . . he assumed she was trembling because he nearly killed her from shock, but part of him wondered if it was more of a flirt. He couldn't help but respond by wrapping his arms around her. It felt good to Jim . . . so natural. He felt Kat reciprocate by holding him closer. One thing became clear: this was not a simple adrenaline rush from a near-death experience.

Kat finally whispered, "I'm glad you came to rescue me . . . even though I didn't need rescuing." Kat giggled.

Jim chuckled in response.

"Maybe you aren't safe, yet."

He could feel Kat softly laugh against his chest yet again. She looked up into his eyes, and he couldn't help but move his hand to lift her chin and gently kiss her lips. To his astonishment and joy, she kissed him back.

Jim slowly pulled away long enough to stroke Kat's hair and touch her cheek with the back of his hand. Her skin was so soft. The slight wrinkles around her eyes were earned with laughter and enjoyment of life, so he decided they were trophies. Kat reached up and ran her hand alongside his jaw and scruffy beard.

Jim extended down and kissed Kat a second time, deep and long. He slid his lips down her neck, kissing carefully and gently. As he started his way back up her neck, he glanced across the room and caught sight of Jax. Jax was sitting in the living room, head tilted in his Aussie shame tilt. He looked disapprovingly at Jim. Jim tried to continue enjoying kissing Kat but kept glancing back to Jax; Jim found himself distracted from the beautiful woman sitting next to him.

Jim waved his hand at Jax behind Kat's back to send him out of the room. Jax responded with another tilt and more disapproval. Jim decided he would shoo Jax away by tossing his hat at him. He quickly and carefully removed his hat and threw it towards Jax like a frisbee. Jax never flinched. He just nonchalantly watched as the hat haphazardly slammed into a terra cotta vase sitting on the end table. The vase wobbled. Jim jumped out of Kat's arms to catch the vase but was too late; the vase hit the floor and smashed into four pieces. Kat, alarmed at Jim's sudden movement and the subsequent crash, looked at Jim.

She laughed, "What in heaven's name are you doing?"

"Well, I was developing performance anxiety because Jax was monitoring us. Then I decided I would shoo him away, but instead I broke your vase. I am so sorry," Jim apologized as he started picking up the pieces. "This is one of the knick-knacks that Dave brought you, isn't it?"

"Yes, yes, it is. But please, don't worry about it. Honestly, it wasn't my favorite, but I didn't have the heart to throw it away," Kat explained.

As Jim picked up the base of the vase, he saw a shiny reflection.

"Well, I guess if you don't care about this," he said as he further broke apart the base.

The shiny element turned out to be a thumbdrive. He held it up to Kat, who looked at it with surprise and curiosity. She quickly scrambled over to Jim on the floor and took it from him.

"Dave brought me this vase the last time I saw him. Let's see what is on this," she said.

Kat scurried over to her desk, turned on a desk lamp, and powered up her laptop.

Jim looked at Jax and said, "You know you ruined a moment for me."

Jax laid his head down and closed his eyes.

"That's right . . . just take a nap."

Kat pulled up the documents on her computer.

"I don't know what any of these things are. They seem so random to me. The first three documents seem to be spreadsheets by different fundraisers, but I think they are true records from AIM Super PAC . . . but I don't know what's important here. The next seven pages seem to be just invitation lists to some of the parties that Sofia and Huck sponsored—notice my name was not on any of those," Kat said sarcastically.

"Oh, now this is interesting. It looks like scanned docs of a few emails from a Tory Hamilton of WHO. Now this may get us somewhere."

Kat quickly glanced through the thread of the email.

"It seems that Dave was interested in the mines of Morocco . . . phosphate mines."

At that statement, Jim quickly became more interested.

"Phosphate? Detective Garringer just mentioned there could be a strange connection of this case with phosphate," Jim said very quietly and very slowly, thinking.

Kat continued, "There is even more about Morocco and those mines. There seems to be an article also written by Tory. Let me read some of this to you:

> *"Morocco produces 50 billion tons of phosphate each year. These mines produce over 70% of the world's usage. Phosphate is then processed into phosphorus and is used in large-scale agriculture. There is more and more demand on phosphate as the world is discovering the green revolution.*
>
> *The United States imports over 43% of U.S. total usage of phosphate from Morocco. New competitors have emerged to raise the price per ton. These competitors are mainly China and India because of their emerging middle class.*
>
> *The purchase and monitoring of all imports are regulated by the U.S. Government Accountability Office."*

"Jim, I'm completely lost. What does this article, the emails from Tory, a list of fundraising donations, and parties have to do with murdering a sweet boy like Dave?"

Kat sat back in her chair, shaking her head. Jim joined with the shake-my-head movement.

"Kat, there seems to be a picture there, as well. Did you open that yet?" Jim asked.

"Oh, no not yet," Kat piped up as she made a few more mouse clicks.

The picture seemed to be a posed picture at Huck's farm. There were only men standing in it.

"The governor . . ." Jim started. "That's Governor Dobbs," he repeated as he pointed to a man in the photo.

Kat nodded her head in agreement.

"Jim, look at the end of the line behind Dobbs," Kat said with a sound of fear in her voice.

Jim located her reference.

"Isn't that one of the guys who hunted me two weeks ago?" Jim asked, also with fear in his voice.

"Yep," Kat responded, never taking her eyes off the screen.

"Who are the other people?" Jim asked.

"I truly don't know," Kat answered.

Jim was already piecing together the GAO statement made during his earlier connection with Ms. Mitchell. He had a very uneasy feeling.

"Kat, I gotta tell you," he started. "I had a conversation with a former Senator, Donna Mitchell, just a couple days ago. I asked her questions about the GAO and the director. I even asked her questions about any connections to Arkansas. I mentioned some mineral transfers that seemed kinda strange. She told me that policy violations could make people wealthy . . . and we know what wealth does to people in power. I think this information confirms what I was telling her."

After what seemed to be ten minutes, but was likely two, Jim stood up and walked toward his gun.

"It's settled. You are not staying here tonight alone," Jim announced.

This time Kat did not argue.

"If you would, please bring the thumbdrive with you; but don't download it to your computer. It could be traced. We can call Detective Garringer on our way back to my cabin. I'll have her meet us there. I can protect us better there," Jim continued as he picked up his gun resting against the wall.

"Ok," Kat agreed, seeing Jim transform into a very serious persona. "Let me send my son a quick note so he won't worry about me; but don't worry: I'll use my bank encrypted email, so no hacking," she said almost laughing at her own cleverness.

After a couple of minutes, she pulled the thumbdrive out, turned off the laptop and lamp, grabbed a few clothes and toiletries, and locked up the cottage. Jax loaded up in the truck when Jim opened the door for Kat.

"No, Big Guy. Tonight you're gonna have to take the back seat," Jim commanded.

Once more, the shame tilt was delivered to Jim; and Jax carefully and slowly crawled into the back seat, eyes squinted.

"Aren't you gonna tell me to load up?" Kat jokingly asked Jim.

"I'm pretty certain you wouldn't respond the same way Jax does," Jim replied as he carefully closed the truck door.

Kat lit up another smile, and Jim trotted over to the driver's side. Soon he had his truck pointed toward Beaver Lake.

Chapter 43

Jim and Kat arrived back to Jim's cabin very late. He didn't have any lights on in his cabin as, again, privacy was his main purpose; so, alerting the human population that his cabin existed never really occurred to him. However, tonight, he was on extra alert. He jumped out of the truck and asked Kat to stay where she was until he turned some lights on.

"Jax, let's go, Boy," Jim commanded.

Jim decided he would have Jax check things out with him. As Jim unlocked the door, he popped on some lights as Jax ran through the house to his corner and sat down next to his food bowl.

"Things must be okay," Jim thought out loud. "A German shepherd would have checked the house out before asking for supper," Jim scolded Jax.

Jax's response was a simple yawn.

Jim returned to the truck and brought Kat into the house. She walked in and slowly took in the surroundings . . . a bachelor pad, without a doubt. But the cabin revealed Jim's character: it was clean but cluttered. Everything was focused on Jim's desire to be in nature. The few photos on the walls were photos, that she guessed, he took himself . . . all of waterfalls. The furniture was sparse but nice.

Jax had his own area. Kat walked over to him and rubbed his ears.

"Is it okay if I stay tonight, Jax?" Kat asked in almost a baby talk.

Jax, loving the attention, closed his eyes and rolled over,

stretching his body out for more petting and possibly a belly rub.

"Yeah, now look who's getting Kat's attention," Jim said sarcastically.

Jim placed Kat's bag in the second bedroom.

As he returned to the kitchen, he asked her, "Can I make you some coffee? I think it will be a long night. Detective Garringer will be here in a couple of hours."

"Sure," Kat responded, still playing with Jax.

She moved over to the couch and stretched out herself.

"So, do you have Netflix?"

"As a matter of fact, I do," Jim answered.

He moseyed over to his recliner and found the remote. He turned on the TV and started to search for Netflix. Kat watched him from the couch, almost laughing at his struggle with technology. Something caught her eye as she watched the screen while Jim fumbled through the channels.

"Jim," Kat spoke inquisitively, "is that the Donna Mitchell you mentioned to me a few hours ago?"

Jim looked up from the remote and saw what Kat was focused on. On the news, they were replaying a press conference where Graham Barnes had decided to step down as comptroller of the General Accountability Office due to "health reasons." He had appointed Donna Mitchell as his successor.

"And we believe that with the election of the next president of the United States, Donna will certainly be confirmed as comptroller for a full term. We are pleased that we could find such a suitable replacement so quickly. I wish her the best of luck, even though she will need none. Congratulations, Donna," Graham wrapped up his speech as he stood behind a podium.

Jim and Kat both watched in silence. This was not what either was expecting.

"Jim, if Graham knows Donna enough to appoint her to this position, is she really a trusted source for us?" Kat asked with a bit of fear in her throat.

"No," Jim answered, still watching the screen as he sat still and numb.

"Kat, I think we have been duped," Jim said as the color started to return to his face. "Donna Mitchell could very well have used what I told her as a tool to force Graham to step down; I don't know." Jim paused for a moment, thinking, before adding, "Or they could just be respected colleagues. Either way, I think we might be in trouble."

Jim reached over to give Kat a hug.

"Don't you fret any," Jim said as he pulled her close. "We will be safe here, and Detective Garringer is also on her way. Honestly, I don't think anyone wants to harm *us*, anyway," Jim continued to reassure Kat.

Just as Jim decided to make a bold move and snuggle up to Kat, he spotted headlights in the distance through his window. Jax awoke and started pacing on alert.

"Just as a precaution I'm gonna get my gun a little closer," Jim said as he stood up to walk back toward the kitchen. Jim took only two steps before the front door exploded open. Jax barked raucously and growled . . . but at what? There seemed to be no one at the door.

The room was suddenly a fury of activity. Three men burst into the cabin. Kat jumped up and instinctively ran toward Jim. He grabbed his shotgun and let out two very quick shots, hitting one man squarely in the chest. The other shot was a miss. But that gave Kat enough time to get behind Jim. Jax stood guard in front of Jim, growling and barking like he was ready to attack, only waiting for the command.

The second man, a small man, who Jim recognized immediately from the pictures and from the hike, pulled a gun and started shooting at Jim. Jim and Kat hunkered down behind the kitchen island, reloading the two guns Jim had with him.

"I know you got information for me," the small man said in broken English. "Tell me where is and who you contacted, and maybe I let you live."

Jim pulled Jax back for fear the assailant would shoot him.

"What information?" Jim asked.

The two remaining men shot four shots into the wall next to Kat and Jim.

"Don't waste time! Where is it?" the man demanded brusquely.

"Okay! Okay!" Jim shouted. "I'll get it for you!"

Kat reached inside her pants pocket and retrieved the thumbdrive.

"Here it is," Jim shouted and tossed it in the air.

Purposely, the toss was high. Just as the third remaining man reached to grab it, Jim jumped up from behind the kitchen island and shot him in the face. The thumbdrive hit the floor and skidded to a halt. The man who was hit by the shotgun blast fell to the ground, bleeding and moaning, then quickly started gasping for air. That lasted only seconds before he fell silent.

The small man fired back. This time the shot found its target through the island and into Kat's shoulder. She screeched and started writhing in pain on the floor. Jim quickly came to her aid and realized the shot was high enough to hopefully have missed all the vital organs.

Suddenly, as he turned back toward the threat remaining in his living room, the small man was almost on top of him. Jax leaped at the man in protective anger. The man threw him down. Jax returned the attack, relentlessly defending his master. As the man aimed his gun and took a shot at Jax, Jim tackled him. Sadly, the bullet found its target in Jax.

Chapter 44

"Oh, hell no!" Jim shouted as he lunged again at the small man who had just shot his dog.

The impact of the man hitting the floor caused him to drop his gun. Jim started punching him as hard as he could. Unfortunately, the man returned the favor. Each blow to Jim's face was excruciating. The man's hands slid to Jim's throat and tightened in a death grip. Jim felt the pressure building in his head; he was losing his breath, as well as his vision. He heard Kat moaning in pain; he saw Jax limp to her side. He didn't know what to do.

A loud moan escaped from the small man who was attempting to choke out Jim. His grip released as he dropped to the ground. Jim gasped for air and tried to make sense of his surroundings. His vision was still blurred. Standing over the small man was a very classy-looking man, holding a gun. Jim started to scramble, but the man held open what was likely a $3,000 suitcoat to show a badge as he laid aside his gun and handcuffed the small man.

"Mr. Cunningham, I'm Brian Pinick. Detective Garringer sent me. Do you know if there are any other perps in the area?"

"No," Jim gasped, choking on gulps of air. "There were only the three. Kat, can you hear me?" Jim uttered.

"Yes," Kat exhaustingly responded.

Jim crawled over to her. There was lots of blood.

"Pinick, we need an ambulance," Jim commanded, panicking at the sight of so much blood.

"On it," Brian said and stepped to the door, phone in hand.

Jim grabbed Kat and held her.

"Is Jax . . . okay?" Kat asked haltingly, not sure if she really wanted to hear the answer.

Jim looked at Jax and saw more blood and noticed Jax panting from pain.

"Jax, come here," Jim commanded.

Jax limped over to his master. Jim quickly ran his hands over Jax's body to find the source of blood. The bullet entered and exited Jax just above his right shoulder. Jim was certain Jax had broken bones; but again, the vital organs seemed untouched.

"Yes, he is okay . . . will need a vet to stitch him up, but he should be okay," Jim responded while quickly rubbing Jax's ears. "Don't worry; the ambulance is on its way. I've got you, Kat," Jim continued as he returned to holding her.

"Mr. Cunningham, do you know what these men were looking for?" Brian interrupted.

"Yes," Jim replied. "They were searching for a thumbdrive we found earlier tonight."

Jim pointed in the direction he last saw the thumbdrive.

As Brian went to pick it up, he asked, "Did you make any copies of the contents on the thumbdrive?"

Jim started to answer, but Kat grabbed his shirt and subtly shook her head. Jim looked into her eyes and understood the message.

"Brian, I don't even know what is on that drive," Jim replied.

Brian shook his head almost disapprovingly as though Jim was insinuating something.

"So, you are saying you never opened the thumbdrive?" Brian continued to inquire, somewhat suspiciously. "Because Detective Garringer told me you had found incriminating evidence involving Governor Dobbs," Brian continued.

Jim looked back to Kat, still bleeding. Realizing that he had never told Detective Garringer anything about the thumbdrive, Jim became incredibly apprehensive.

"When will that ambulance get here, Brian?" Jim asked.

"Mr. Cunningham, you didn't answer my question: did you open the thumbdrive?" Brian repeated very sternly.

At that point Jim realized Brian had likely not called for an ambulance. The small man on the floor seemed to be coming around but was bound by handcuffs. Brian had picked up his weapon. Jim knew he had to get Kat to the hospital . . . and soon.

"No, Brian, I did not open the thumbdrive," Jim replied.

"You see, Mr. Cunningham, I don't know that I believe you," Brian said slowly drawing out each word.

As he spoke, he recovered the thumbdrive from the floor. He placed it into his pocket and then moved closer to Jim and Kat.

Suddenly, lights shown through the kitchen window. They could hear footsteps running toward the cabin. Brian moved quickly to the window and recognized the owner of the footsteps.

As Detective Garringer neared the door, Brian shouted, "It's all clear, Lori."

Detective Garringer quickly and cautiously, as training had taught her, stepped inside the cabin door . . . or what was left of it.

Just as she started to lower her gun to its holster, Jim yelled, "Careful, Lori; he is one of them."

Lori started to react, but it was too late; Brian had his gun on her.

"Brian?" Detective Garringer quizzed. "What are you doing?"

"Lori, don't take this the wrong way; I just need to protect my employer. These suits are not cheap," Brian said laughingly. "Now, let's get down to business."

Brian dropped the thumbdrive to the floor and destroyed it with his overpriced shoes.

"I really don't care what was on there, because it is gone now. I know these two," he said as he waved his gun back and forth between Jim and Kat, "didn't email it to anyone because I hacked both their email accounts a month ago."

"Brian, I still don't understand. What are you planning to do here tonight?" Lori pressed.

"I'm going to erase a problem," Brian responded. "I don't care what each of you know because it ends here tonight."

Just as Brian had started his monologue, Jim realized that for once he was carrying his concealed weapon. Without thinking, he lowered Kat down to the floor, rose to his knees, and pulled out his gun. He shot twice. Sadly, each shot was a miss. However, as the distracted Brian moved to get a shot off at Jim, he was too slow. With the first fidget of distraction, Detective Garringer placed two shots directly into Brian's heart. His body crumpled before her. In shock, she stood over his body, gun still aimed at his chest. All the training she had had did not prepare her for protecting herself from an old love.

Detective Garringer shook the reality off her. She kicked the gun away from Brian's side and ran to Jim and Kat. Realizing Kat needed an ambulance sooner rather than later, she immediately radioed for backup and an ambulance.

Dejectedly, Jim revealed, "The thumbdrive is destroyed, and we didn't make any copies."

Jim had resumed holding Kat and would not let go but was trying to catch up Detective Garringer on recent events.

"It's okay, Professor. As long as you two . . . I mean three," she said, looking at a wounded Jax, "are okay."

The ambulance and backup arrived in a blaze of glory in about 15 minutes. Sirens and lights lit up Jim's very private world. The EMTs quickly responded to Kat's injury and assured Jim she would be okay and was safe now.

_____ Chapter 45

Toby stepped into his cabin. He was alone. Nobody knew about this cabin or, obviously, knew he was there. Toby had managed to allude his security staff but was certain they were already looking for him. When he had become aware of the chain of events going down and saw the announcement of Donna Mitchell, Toby knew he was in trouble. He needed peace and quiet to rethink and strategize how he was going to handle this situation—how he was going to survive.

Toby stepped into the small kitchen and poured a whiskey . . . straight. This was not going to be the night of sipping alcohol for prosperity. Tonight, he needed to numb his senses so he could think.

Not even his wife, the shrew, knew where he was. In fact, she didn't even know this cabin existed. Toby was careful about who knew. He had a cleaning lady who came out once a week to clean and stock the cabinets. She was under the impression the cabin was owned by a trucking tycoon from Alabama.

Toby finished the drink, then poured another. He peered out the window. The snow fell heavy here in Colorado Springs. He reminisced about the years of hiking through the snow, hunting elk. In those days, hunting was less monitored. He could easily escape, hunt, and return to the office renewed. At some point, he remembered he had hoped to bring his daughter with him some time. However, she and her mother did not seem to embrace the country life. Their idea of a retreat involved a beach, great service, and sleeping all day. He silently wished he had had a son.

But today was different. No hunting on this trip. He stood

there, mindlessly tossing a coin up and down as he tried to think.

The trick to staying vibrant in the political realm was staying one move ahead of the competition. In this case, the competitors were starting to stack up.

"Why hasn't anyone called yet?" Toby thought to himself.

He needed to know the collateral damage from tonight. That information would put his strategy into motion.

He received the call he was dreading. The call marked the end of his political career, as well as posed a risk to his very life. Toby sat the phone on the counter. He dropped the coin. It landed logo side up, representing the Old Dominion emblem. He stared at the emblem. This was a sign. He took a deep breath. He decided it was time to defend himself. He headed to the closet where he kept his guns. He reached in for his rifle and started rummaging for ammunition.

Toby heard a car door shut. He was startled. His search for ammunition escalated. He tossed boxes on the floor, searching for the right caliber. He found it. Toby fumbled the box open as he heard the cabin door open. Toby's face drained of color. He was full of fear. He turned to face the would-be assailant. He relaxed some.

"I can reason or negotiate with *you*," Toby thought.

Chapter 46

Jim and Detective Garringer both arrived at the hospital coffee counter at the same time early the next morning, having never left the hospital. That arrival made both of them chuckle.

"Professor Cunningham," Detective Garringer greeted him.

"Detective Garringer," Jim responded, smiling.

After a few seconds of awkward silence while they awaited the barista's gift of caffeine, they gave each other a quick embrace.

"I hear Kat's son is arriving here later this morning. I know she is ready for some normalcy and certainly any time with her boys," Detective Garringer offered.

"Yes, it's been a strange 12 hours. The only thing that still bothers me . . . really Kat and I . . . is that there was something on that thumbdrive that cost Dave his life and almost all of ours," he said as he drew an imaginary circle with his finger, indicating the group involved in the case. "And we can't even direct you to what that is."

"It's okay," Detective Garringer assured. "Trust me, criminals have a way of declaring themselves."

They both took a sip of coffee and grimaced as the coffee was not up-to-standard. They walked back to Kat's room. Detective Garringer entered first and saw Kat bandaged and IV-upped. Kat had regained her color and snarky sense of humor.

"I'm in a hospital less than four hours, and you already find a beautiful woman to replace me," Kat joked while holding out her hand toward Jim.

Jim laughed and went to her side, giving Kat a little kiss on the cheek.

"Well, well," Detective Garringer muttered, "what's going on here?"

Detective Garringer raised her eyebrow as she had been unaware of the budding romance between the two. Before either could answer her question, Detective Garringer received a call. Upon realizing from whom the call was, she quickly answered it without excusing herself; however, she stepped outside of the room for privacy. As she listened to the person relay the news on the other end of the line, Detective Garringer's face turned as white as a sheet.

Stepping around the detective to get into the room was a young blonde man who Jim recognized from Kat's pictures.

"You must be Kat's son, Grant?" Jim started, holding his hand out in a friendly manner.

"That's me . . . the *favorite* son," Grant responded in a teasing mode, giving Jim's offered hand a firm shake.

Jim noted the same snarky sense of humor. Grant leaned down and hugged his mother with force. He stroked her hair out of her face.

"You okay, Mom?" he asked warmly.

"Of course. I've always said men have bad aim," Kat joked.

She and Grant were busy reconnecting when Detective Garringer walked back into the room and stared at the scene.

"And you are Grant, CIA analyst?" Detective Garringer inquired with a large smile on her face.

"CIA?" Jim asked, stunned. "You said he worked for the state," Jim said to Kat accusingly.

"Did I lie?" Kat responded.

"Would you like to catch them up on what's going down right now?" Detective Garringer smugly asked Grant.

Grant chuckled as he responded in true generation-Y style, "Sure! When I received Mom's email yesterday from her bank email address, I knew something was wrong, as well as urgent, as she is strict about email rules of mixing personal and professional emails. She had attached some documents for me to review. My job is to monitor chatter from Western Sahara. I knew immediately who all the people were; I just had no idea *how* they were connected. The invitation lists showed that Governor Dobbs, Graham Barnes, and Bin Moussir attended many parties together. The emails and article from Tory showed that Dave had figured out a connection to phosphate; to Huck Ferguson, the commodity broker; to Bin Moussir, the owner of the phosphate mines; and to Graham Barnes, the comptroller general of the Government Accountability Office. The Super PAC accounting actually showed the large sums of money coming into Sofia Agassi's campaign for Governor Dobbs' presidential campaign. Once I pieced that together from the documents, it was easy to track the money to know what was going on.

"Governor Dobbs repaid the favor in many ways. One was to get the U.S. Accountability Office off Bin's back since the phosphate is mined by slave labor. That, of course, is against U.S. law. And second, because the U.S. was able to obtain unlimited phosphate, which is a limited resource here, to help Huck to trade in it and make huge commissions. But more concerning was the need to find out if the phosphate was being stockpiled somewhere for terrorist activity.

"So basically, I have been monitoring some of them from afar. I knew Mom was likely in trouble when I understood what she had. I couldn't reach her because I guess she was with you," Grant paused and glanced accusingly at Jim.

Jim was unprepared for Kat's adult son to scold him for his romantic interest in his mother. That made Jim uncomfortable, and the fact this kid was a CIA agent made him just a little nervous.

"The CIA agents discovered the chatter of what happened at your cabin . . . which, by the way, I want to talk to you about," again peering directly at Jim. "Taking my mother to a cabin that I know nothing about . . ." Grant started again, starring at Jim in protective mode. "Then we deployed agents to make arrests, find out where my mom was, and contact Detective Garringer. Oh . . . and let's not forget Brian! Brian was on Governor Dobbs' payroll, and we've known that for a short time. He helped make problems for Dobbs go away for years. We assume that if Dobbs won the presidency, Brian would be recommended to be the next FBI Director.

"Currently, Sofia Agassi has been arrested as an accessory to the murder of Dave Reid and for treason. I just received word that Sofia is cooperating with our agents.

"Also, Governor Dobbs has been tracked down via GPS on his phone by his security detail. He was at his cabin in Colorado Springs. Before stepping into this room, the agents reported they did find a body at the cabin. They presume it is that of Governor Dobbs but will make that declaration shortly. He had written a suicide note claiming responsibility for the murder of Dave Reid, then apparently took his own life via a gun shot. The quirky thing about the gun shot is that it was from his right hand. Governor Dobbs is left-handed. So, that investigation has officially started.

"As far as Graham Barnes . . . we also have arrested him, but I don't think that arrest is going to stick. We really have no real evidence against him. He's a tool. Our best effort to prove Graham's guilt is if we can locate Bin Moussir and get sworn testimony from him. But again, Moussir is not a U.S. citizen; so, that may not be damning enough."

Jim and Kat sat there, consuming all the information that Grant just relayed. Detective Garringer had obviously been given more information as she did not exhibit any shock from Grant's news.

Grant was finished explaining the new information. He got up and walked over to Jim. Jim was somewhat in shock mode, so he didn't know what to do . . . but he wasn't ready to let go of Kat's hand just yet.

Grant reached out and shook Jim's hand again as he spoke, "We're cool, Brother. Thanks for looking out for my mom."

Jim was relieved and smiled his crooked grin. His heart started beating a normal beat again.

Kat smiled her drugged smile at both of them. Then she startled everyone and caught attention. The tone of her voice caused them to believe her pain had escalated.

"What about Jax?" she squeaked.

"Is there another man I don't know anything about?" Grant said in a condemning voice.

"No, Jax is my dog . . . my best friend, actually," Jim quickly responded. "After I got your mom into the ambulance last night, Detective Garringer gave Jax and I a police escort to a vet on standby. Apparently, he is the best, as he is the canine unit number one vet. I haven't heard from him this morning, as I was torn between staying with Jax and staying with your mom. Detective Garringer promised me she would keep me posted. Any news, Detective?" Jim asked glancing back toward her.

"Yes, as a matter of fact, there is some good news. Jax's gun shot was a clean through-and-through shot. No broken bones, but some very bad and deep bruising. In fact, it's interesting you brought that up just at this point because someone has been waiting to see all of you."

The detective stepped over to the door and held it open as in trotted Jax, tired, moving slowly, bandaged, and wearing a bandana with a police ribbon for Exercising Courage Under Pressure attached. Jax moved as fast as he could while Jim bolted toward him. Jax snuggled into Jim, and Jim held him as tightly as he dared. Jim then gingerly picked him up and, as Jax was a big dog, clumsily brought him close to Kat. Kat reached out and stroked Jax with one hand. Detective Garringer then instructed the vet attendant to take Jax back to the special waiting area so the nurses wouldn't get upset.

"Now we all begin to heal," she spoke quietly.

 Chapter 47

The day was brutally cold . . . more bitter and colder than any day Jim could remember. The ground was frozen hard and covered sparingly with snow and sleet. He stood next to the grave, his head wilting downward as the preacher spoke. The words filtered through the air in a hush.

The solemn occasion was conflicting. Obviously, the celebration of a person passing from this Earth is saddening. Everyone there certainly had a part of their soul die at this very moment. Yet, the closure this moment offered to Dave's family and, especially, to Megan was surprisingly comforting. This was that moment they never were able to achieve in the past: they finally had the opportunity to say "Good-bye; we love you; and we will miss you."

Jim watched Kat, who stood to his right, as she breathed heavily in an effort to prevent the tears.

"Why?" he thought to himself. "This is the time to let tears flow. Tears are welcomed here today as they are certainly a display of love . . . *deep* love."

As he tilted his head in order to see Kat's expression, she looked up into his calming smile. Jim's smile was one of compassion, the expression Kat needed at that moment.

To Kat's right was Grant, as well as her other son who flew in for the funeral as they considered Megan family. Grant stood completely still and motionless. He had accepted Dave's disappearance years ago. However, today was the certainty of the end of Dave's life. This acquiescence of the moment seemed to weigh heavily on him.

Opposite them, across the casket stood Megan, Dave's mother, and Dave's brother, Jeff. Dave's mother had cried for ten years; yet she still cried. Her chest heaved under the pressure of the moment. Jeff reached out to hold her and comfort her through this moment.

At the far end of the casket stood Detective Garringer . . . stoically . . . an embodiment of the agency.

The preacher finished his prayer, "We ask for comfort for the family and the loved ones as Dave so intensely loved so many people in this world. Amen."

Kat reached out and held Jim's hand. Jim watched the few people hug and support Dave's mother. He couldn't help but notice that Dave deserved so much more than this. Dave had worked to help people. He had protected Megan. Dave's legacy was erased from him by greed and power. Yes, Dave deserved more than this.

Grant touched Kat's shoulder and mentioned that he and his brother were going over to speak with Megan.

Detective Garringer walked gingerly over the frozen ground to Jim and Kat.

"Kat, I'm very sorry this ended the way it has. I know this has been a bit of an adventure for you, and I'm very sorry for that," Detective Garringer offered.

Kat responded by reaching up and hugging Detective Garringer. Somewhat caught off guard, she hesitated, then fell into the embrace and returned the affection while soaking up the strength that was offered. A mother's love was transmitted in that hug. The hug represented so much more to Detective Garringer.

During the embrace, Kat whispered, "I am proud of you, Lori. Remember, there is strength in letting go."

Detective Garringer's eyes opened, and she starred across Kat's shoulder. That was exactly what she had been doing: holding onto the past. How could Kat have known that?

Everyone dispersed from the cemetery and carefully drove away on the icy roads. Hours later, Detective Garringer arrived at her apartment. She walked in and hung her coat on the coatrack nestled by the front door. As she tossed her keys on the entry table, she caught a glimpse of the shadowbox.

She stared into the box: one dull, bronze medal as a token of her past.

She started to smile as she spoke to the shadowbox, "This time I won, and I will continue to win. Time to let go of the past."

Detective Garringer straightened her back, held her head a little higher than before, and walked through to the living room.

"Mr. Barnes, you are next," she said while opening her laptop with a confident and snarky smirk.

About the Author

Sheila Webb Pierson is an economist who grew up on a dairy farm in northeast Oklahoma and northwest Arkansas which, according to her, is why her sense of reality is greatly distorted. Her most prestigious awards range from the Tulsa State Fair Supreme Champion Guernsey to the Arkansas State FFA Parliamentary Procedure Champion Team . . . yes, she is a true country gal.

Sheila entered corporate America and has been in the business of conducting leadership initiatives for several companies including Fortune 100 companies, resulting in the launch of her first published work, Coveralls and Tell-Alls: Everything You Need to Know About Leadership I Learned on a Farm.

Sheila keeps returning to her two loves: her farm and her fascination with storytelling. As a requested professional speaker, she receives accolades regarding her ability to mesmerize her audience with good, southern-style humor and messaging. She is often requested to translate southern jargon for those less educated, bless their hearts.

Often fueled by chocolate and a slight sweet tea addiction, she finds joy and solace on her farm where she continues to be trained by her small pack of Aussies . . . her progress is outstanding!